Chapter One

It is said that silence can be deafening, b₁
simply allows other, previously hidden sounds, to make an entrance, occupying the space freed by the absence and making our ears more sensitive to these hidden noises? The last time a car had passed the house was nearly 10 minutes ago. The sudden crunch as the driver dropped the gears to navigate the sleeping policeman had startled James. But this wasn't the car he was expecting, far too soon. Up until that point, his aural focus was on his deep breathing, the hum of the TV in standby mode, and the irregular dripping of the tap in the kitchen, each drop plinking as it hit the soapy water.

The room was lit by a standing lamp, the result of a recent trip to Ikea. It looked great in the store, but once assembled at home, it looked a bit wonky, slightly leaning to one side. Two months later it blended in nicely, just like the thousands of identical lamps in living rooms across the country. The rest of the room was made up of furniture from various chains, an attempt to create a unique living experience spoiled by the fact that most visitors would recognise at least one item from their own abode. James wasn't overly keen on furniture or decor, this was Sally's department.

Until then, he was blissfully unaware of his surroundings, his previous focus was limited to the space between his chair and the TV. As he sat staring at the room, he became conscious of the colour and texture of the sofa opposite. The curtains drawn behind the sofa were bunched, he had contemplated getting up and adjusting them, but, as the minutes passed, he tried to ignore them. He had bigger problems to contemplate.

He had made the phone call from his mobile four minutes ago, just after midnight. He didn't want to make the call any earlier as it would have spoiled his birthday. It hadn't been the best birthday, but it was his birthday all the same.

A friend had told him a few months earlier that fewer than four police cars routinely patrol Sussex after midnight. Would they alert one of the cars currently roaming Hastings or Brighton? Or would they dispatch one of the idle vehicles parked outside of the night station? If they were sent from John Street in Brighton, it would take around 20 minutes to reach his house in Offham. He looked at the time on his phone and contemplated what more he could do with the remaining ten minutes. He couldn't think of anything useful, so just sat there in calm contemplation.

Sally, his wife of 16 years, sat in the chair opposite, her eyes, which had earlier judged him, were covered by a blanket draped over her body. The blood stain had slowly moved down the covering, but was still some way off reaching the end that hovered inches from the carpet. Would the blood make a sound as it splashed against the thick wool carpet? Given the ten minutes that remained, he doubted that he would find out.

The phone call was short and perfunctory. The initial response of the dispatcher was one of confusion, most pubs had closed just over an hour before, maybe the caller was inebriated? The temptation was to ask a few more questions to determine if the call was genuine, but that wasn't their job. James was very direct in his statement, and it wasn't their decision, so they promptly transferred the call.

Chris had drawn the short straw, it was his turn to man the phones overnight. A half drunk cup of coffee beside the phone had turned cold, he was planning the short trip to the kitchen to top it up with something fresher and hotter when the phone rang.

"This is Detective Thomas; how can I help you?"

2

"Detective?" James was expecting a duty PC to take the call, he had been escalated to a detective already, his message was clearer than he thought.

"Detective, I have just killed my wife Sally, I think you should come over."

"Pardon, could you say that again please?" Although Chris had heard the words quite clearly, he wanted to be sure.

"Detective Thomas, I have killed my wife. Sally is sitting on the armchair in front of me, very dead. Can you come to my house in Offham, near Lewes?"

James went on to confirm his address.

Chapter Two

Saturday 01:05

Sally had just received the text message, "Pissed, pick me up, at HH now."

The initial relief, she had pondered the 'where the fuck is he?' question for the past few hours, was soon replaced by frustration that she would have to drag herself out of the house to collect James, not even a 'please' in his request.

She was also angry that she would have to wait until he woke up to question him about the accounting anomaly she discovered earlier. The deadline to submit the company accounts was Tuesday. She had been chasing him for details for the past few months, and discrepancies like this one would only increase the pressure. Her social diary was, in her words, shot to shit for the past few weeks, and a planned meal with her friend Carol for Tuesday was looking unlikely.

The drive to Cooksbridge station was only 5 minutes, the train would take around 15 minutes from Haywards Heath. She decided against changing out of her pyjamas, picked up the keys, and walked out to the car in her slippers. The air was still as she drove along the quiet lanes. She drove over the level crossing and parked up by the platform exit.

How many times had she made this journey unplanned like this? As a permanent servant to her husband, there had to be more to life than making his meals, sorting the kids and picking him up inebriated at all times of the day? But life was comfortable, a lovely home, the kids happy in their school, and, recently, her new role as company secretary at her husband's company, Brunswick Haulage.

She was able to do the job entirely from home, James insisted, describing the office there as no more than a portacabin infested by mice. The documents would be emailed to her, all she had to do was consolidate the details and keep the books up to date. The salary was great, apparently overgenerous, but she wasn't complaining about a bit of nepotism if it favoured her.

When she took over the books, they were a mess, with receipts and invoices missing, but James was always able to find the document, taking a picture on his phone and emailing it to her. With access to the books from previous years, she was able to draw on earlier losses and offset these against the substantial profits from recent years. The books from seven years ago showed a small company living one week to the next, and then the sudden boom in business three years ago when new contracts resulted in an expansion of the fleet. Small business owners describe their experience as feast or famine, Sally recalled the famine of four years ago, when they lived in a small flat in Lewes, and compared it with the relative feast of today, living in their dream house.

The silence was abruptly broken as the lights on the level crossing flashed, accompanied by a loud ringing, a warning to motorists, cyclists, and pedestrians that a train was approaching. She watched as the barriers lowered and listened carefully for the London train in the distance. The hiss on the line as the train approached.

Two minutes later the barriers were raised, and Sally started the drive to Lewes, muttering.

"Arseholes!"

In the day, the Victoria trains ran twice an hour and only stopped at

Cooksbridge every other one. The train that James had boarded was one of those that didn't stop. Of course, it was the last train out of London, this never stops at Cooksbridge. No doubt James would find the whole episode hilarious. As she drove into Lewes wearing her pyjamas, she wasn't laughing. She drove to the front of the station, no sight of James. She picked up her phone and dialled him, no response, so she drove around and into the station carpark. Again, no sign. Her phone rang.

"You never guess what happened?" James was slurring his words, she had guessed, but let him talk regardless.

"You never guess what? The train didn't stop at Cooksbridge and I'm at Lewes now," his voice echoed the hilarity that he imagined of his situation.

"I did guess James, where the fuck are you? I'm in the car park. I can't see you."

"Oh, you're here already. I thought I had time for a quick one. I'm at Platform 6," The Lansdown Arms was signed as Platform 6 as the adjunct to the five platforms at Lewes station. Few locals referred to the pub as platform 6, but James found it amusing and insisted on doing so, always having to explain the reason.

"Oh, for fucks sake. Drink up, I'll be there in 30 seconds."

Sally turned the car around and drove up the ramp. A small crowd of people stood outside drinking, she looked for James and couldn't see him and was just about to call again when he walked out of the pub bearing two glasses. He walked over to the car.

"I got you one as well, lockup the car and join us."

6

"I'm in my pyjamas. Drink up, otherwise you'll be walking home. I'm not joking James."

James stood looking at Sally, he felt himself sway and quickly moved one foot forward to catch himself, splashing the beer as he did. He opened his mouth as if to request a reprieve, quickly realising the futility of trying.

"Ok, two secs..

He drained the first glass in one go, swallowed and belched, paused for a few seconds, and downed half of the second glass. He turned on his heel and walked back to the pub, placed the empty glass on the table and quickly finished the remains of the second glass. He returned to the car and got in the passenger seat.

"Seemed a shame to waste it," he belched again as he spoke.

Sally rammed the car into first and hit the throttle as the car sped up Station Street, over the crossing and down Fisher Street. She turned sharply left and sped up Whitehill towards the Offham road, throwing James from side to side.

'Serve him right if he throws up', she thought to herself. Then she slowed down.

"You can throw up in your car, but not mine," Sally spoke the words in frustration to James.

She used the controls to wind down the passenger window and pushed him so his face was outside the car.

❖

James was snoring, this was was hardly surprising considering the amount he had drunk the night before. Sally had long since given up trying to sleep beside him, it had felt like Chinese water torture as she waited for the next grunt to shatter the silence. She had moved to one of the kids' beds and slept soundly. Now downstairs, she could hear the rumble as grunts and snores settled into a more rhythmic routine, she was unlikely to see him anytime soon.

She was still pondering the issue that she had encountered the day before with the accounts. The haulage business had been hugely successful over the previous three years, so much so that they had increased the fleet of vehicles from two to six and used an agency for the extra drivers needed to keep the trucks moving. More vehicles mean more services, MOTs, fuel, tolls, and other costs. The extra drivers meant an increase in agency fees from the initial requirement of six to twenty today. The numbers were high and the increase in accounting effort also grew. The more a company turned over, the closer the authorities took an interest, like the Mafia, who took a percentage of the companies it 'protected', the Inland Revenue wanted their protection money as well.

The six trucks that worked mostly around the clock incurred huge costs, by the time that service, rental, depreciation, and fuel costs were taken into account, the profit margin was low. Thankfully, James had managed keep the trucks moving regularly, so these small margins were able to add up.

Sally had ordered and catalogued the piles and piles of receipts so that any queries from the authorities could be quickly answered. Each year the vehicles had to undergo an MOT, and she had created a file with the certificates, going back in time. The recent acquisitions had only three certificates, but the existing fleet of two had paperwork going back eight years. Her OCD side appreciated the consistent form size as she inserted them into plastic folders that were then stored in the folder marked 'MOTs'. This uniformity of the form spotlighted the problem as she carefully ordered the certificates by year.

As a company secretary, responsible for the accounts, Sally was only interested in the money side. The service details, such as parts and labour, were the responsibility of the fleet manager, a role undertaken by James. In the centre of the MOT document is an entry for mileage. Running a haulage business profitably meant that the lorries were constantly on the road and moving. The first few years of business showed annual mileage of around 40,000. By the time the fleet was expanded, the initial two vehicles had covered more than 200,000 miles. But, for the past two years, the mileage had increased by barely 1,000 miles. If the business was idle, this wouldn't register, but the pile of fuel receipts and invoices for jobs completed told a different story.

She was sure that there was some sensible explanation, if the accounts were not due in three days, she might have let it slip for a short while, but an answer was urgently needed.

Sally had given up on the noise coming from upstairs and taken her coffee out into the garden, where the sound of nature, occasionally interrupted by a passing car, made for a more pleasant tune. The first she heard from James was as he walked into the garden with two cups of coffee.

"Good morning darling. Sorry about last night's little adventure," he bent down and kissed her, breathing beer fumes in her face, and passed her the fresh coffee.

Sally looked at her watch, 9.30a.m. She wasn't expecting to see him this side of midday.

Sally looked stern. A marriage is made up of small indiscretions, no one can be perfect all of the time, but there's no harm in twisting the knife for a few minutes, she thought.

"I'm not clearing up the sick, that's your problem."

James looked horrified, had he really been sick on the way home. He couldn't recall much of the journey, save the roller coaster ride as he was thrown about through the bendy roads. He looked to Sally, the serious look on her face.

She couldn't keep the act up any longer, the seriousness turned into a smile and then a laugh.

"You were lucky this time, you managed to get out of the car and upstairs. Just! Why do you drink so much?"

James knew it was a rhetorical question, one he asked himself so many times, one that he couldn't answer.

"It was just a few drinks with friends," as he spoke the words he could see Sally's serious face appear again.

"OK, maybe more than a few drinks. But it was all business, darling. We have a new contract and need to acquire two more trucks. Things are on the up."

James was expecting the serious face to break back into a smile, but Sally just stood up and walked indoors. He pondered his last few words. Had he said something wrong? He looked up and could see Sally in her office. Two minutes later she came downstairs and back into the garden.

"I'm a bit confused by these," as Sally spoke she passed James the folder marked MOTs, he looked confused.

"It's my filing. I know these are not totally necessary for the accounts, but I like to keep full records. I'm confused by DZ and SU"

The references were to the last two digits of the registration number, all six trucks had unique prefixes and were referred to in this way. One day there may be a duplication, but this was some way off.

"What about DZ and SU?," James was not sure where this was going and the residue alcohol from the night before wasn't helping.

"It's the mileage, for the past two years, they have barely changed"

"Oh, yes. Well, DZ and SU are the oldest trucks in the fleet. We tend to use the newer trucks for the long journeys, so the mileage doesn't change that much," James started to think on his feet. He looked at Sally for a change in her demeanour but didn't see any; instead she looked more serious.

"That doesn't add up, I have diesel receipts and service invoices. Also these trucks have been booked against jobs for pretty much every day over the last two years," Sally made clear that she wasn't buying the simple explanation.

James didn't have an immediate answer, he could see Sally's confused look. How to fob her off while he developed a more plausible excuse?

"I see what you're saying. Can I pop over to the yard this afternoon and check? Maybe there is an issue with the equipment? I'm sure we have tachographs that will show the mileage," James tried to make as plausible and argument as possible, internally praying that would work.

"OK, but can you make sure it is this afternoon? The reports need to be filed on Tuesday, and I'm the company secretary so it's me they will chase."

"Of course. I will pop there straight away," James looked at Sally as her smile returned

"Not straight away," she said, passing James a small box wrapped in a bow. "Happy Birthday, darling."

His head was still throbbing, and he had forgotten the day. He must be getting old when he can't remember that it's his own birthday.

"Aw, thank you," he took the small box, carefully removed the bow (unsure why he needed to remove it carefully, it would be in the rubbish bin within five minutes) and opened it. It was an antique Rolex.

"Thank you." He started to remove the iWatch from his wrist, but Sally stopped him.

"Whoah! For the amount that cost me, I can't afford for you to be wearing it," she smiled as she spoke, "especially when you are a bit unstable on your feet. Leave it until later."

He handed her the box with the watch still in place. She picked up the bow and walked into the kitchen, dropping the bow in the bin placing the watch on the side in the kitchen.

James' thoughts returned to the previous conversation, he needed to talk to Kevin quickly. He dug into his pocket for his phone and sent him a text.

'Problem. Can you meet me at the cafe for 11?"

Thirty seconds passed and then he sensed the vibration of his iWatch.

'Sure, what type of problem?'

'Bad', he replied.

He put the phone back into his pocket

Sally came back outside with two glasses of orange juice and croissants.

"I think I will head over to the yard now and check out those records, if that's OK?"

"No it's not, let's enjoy your birthday breakfast first of all. Anyhow, your car is still at Cooksbridge, I need to get ready so I can take you there to collect it."

James concurred. Take some time out for now.

James stared at his watch, he caught Sally's eye as he did this, and he considered how it was impossible to check the time without someone noticing. The time was 10.15 a.m., he had arranged to meet Charles for 11 a.m. He would be pushed to get to Cooksbridge to collect his car and then get to Brighton for 11 a.m.

Sally sensed his impatience and was just about to speak when James started.

"Look, I feel I need to get a start on those mileage details. You've only got until Tuesday, I don't want to see you fined or imprisoned," he looked over at Sally smiling, the prison suggestion was a joke, both knew a late return was not that serious. He expected her to return the smile, she looked more serious.

"What is it, James? It's your birthday and you look as though your thoughts are all over the place."

"Oh, it's nothing. Just a mixture of the hangover and the worries about meeting the new contract. I'm sure that it will pass," he said trying to change the subject. "Are we going out tonight?"

Sally suspected something wasn't right, but decided to let it pass. "I thought an evening in would be better, it will be such a lovely night to be in the garden. I have ordered a takeaway for 7 p.m."

"That sounds like a great idea," the smile on his face failed to hide the worry in his eyes.

"Give me 20 minutes, I'll pop for a quick shower, and then I can drop you off at Cooksbridge to collect your car. Hopefully, once the paperwork is clear, we can relax for your birthday?"

"Great idea."

Sally stood up and headed upstairs. James waited, staring at the window, watching as her silhouette undressed and walked into the bathroom. He stood up and walked indoors and grabbed her keys from the hook. He clicked the remote to open the door, started the engine, and drove off.

James drove his car up to the junction, indicating left to turn towards Lewes. He looked at the clock, 10.25 a.m., 35 minutes to get to

Brighton. It would be marginally quicker to go via Lewes and along the A27, but he needed some space to clear his mind before meeting Kevin. He flipped the indicator and turned right along the Chailey road, turning left shortly afterwards towards Ditchling. The sun was still rising, and it occasionally shone in his rearview mirror as the car navigated the sweeping turns. He instinctively turned down Underhill Road, the short cut to Ditchling Beacon, but immediately regretted the decision as he was forced to stop for three oncoming cars, having to reverse at one stage.

As the car reached the beacon, he felt refreshed by the open road with the Downs on three sides and the Brighton seafront ahead of him. He was sure he could find a way out of this, Kevin was a clever guy.

His watch vibrated, he looked at the face as the message appeared.

'Have you just driven off? What the fuck is happening, James?', no kisses. No time to reply just yet, he thought.

He drove past the Ship Hotel on the seafront, turned right and parked the car.

When most people suggest they meet in 'the cafe' the destination is usually some cute independent boutique operation, but Kevin and James had settled on Starbucks as 'the cafe' sometime back. James started to queue for a drink, when he noticed Kevin signalling him, he walked over and sat down.

"Black Americano, and I got you a caramel slice, sorry it's not a cake. Happy birthday."

"Thank you." James compared his own tracksuit and tee-shirt with Kevin's debonair look, smart chinos, an open neck shirt and a cravat.

This was dress down for Kevin, he couldn't imagine him in a tee-shirt, let alone tracksuit bottoms. If he was to visit Glastonbury, he would be wearing a tie.

"My pleasure. So what's the problem? Not like you to be so short in your message."

And just like you to be so direct, thought James.

"Sally has uncovered a hole in the accounts. It's so fucking obvious that I am amazed we, sorry YOU, missed it. How many more holes will there be? I told you I wasn't happy with this, but you insisted, all will be OK." James couldn't hold back, the words were clear and his manner matched them.

"Calm down, dear chap. There's nothing we can't sort out. Tell me, what's the issue?" The contrast between the two - James shaking as he blurted out the problems and Kevin, carefully dabbing his lips with a tissue as he drank his latte.

"It's the mileage. The whole thing is falling apart. How did you not think of this? The fucking mileage."

"Dear, dear. I asked you to calm down, please take me through this. There is always an answer." Again, Kevin remained calm as he spoke.

James started to explain, with Kevin regularly stopping him as he raced ahead.

"Ok, let me think. Drink your coffee, the answer always lies at the bottom of a beer glass. He stood up and signalled James to follow, James lifted the cup to his lips, he hadn't drunk a drop, and the coffee was cold.

❖

They walked the short distance to the Druids Head, Kevin signalled to James to grab a seat while he walked to the bar to order the drinks.

He passed James the pint of lager, smiling. James leaned forward and swapped it for the pint of bitter. A long running joke between them, it helped alleviate the tension.

James lifted the glass to his lips, tasted the drink, and then took two large mouthfuls, placing the half empty glass back on the table. For a couple of minutes, they sat in silence, considering their predicament. The pub had only opened 45 minutes before but was already filling up with weekend crowds.

His watch vibrated again, he looked at the face and saw an incoming call from Sally. He pressed the decline button.

"What's Sally like?" Kevin's question broke the silence.

"What do you mean, what's Sally like? You want to know her temperament? Whether she gives to charity? What is she like in bed? Come to the point, Kevin, I have just driven out on her in a fucking panic."

"I mean would she understand?" Kevin remained calm realising that this was the only way to get through to James.

"Understand what? Where has the money been coming from for the past three years? No she fucking wouldn't!"

"Calm down, James; we will find a solution. We won't if you can't calm down."

James grabbed the beer and downed the remaining half pint in a single gulp. He stood up, walked to the bar, and ordered two more beers. He returned to the table, sipping his.

"So, what's the answer? I've given you 5 minutes, you seem so cock-sure that we would find the answer in the bottom of a pint glass. Well, I've got to the bottom of mine and it's no clearer. Do you want me to keep drinking on the off chance?"

Kevin stared at James, it was pointless trying to talk to him, wait for the beer to relax him. Although James was just sipping, the sips were constant, and he could see the level dropping faster than a barometer in a storm. He stood up and walked to the bar, returning two minutes later with a fresh pint to replace the already empty glass.

"We're going to have to see Sally and talk this through. Hopefully she values what this deal has given you and the family. I'm sure she will see sense."

James nodded, the beer was relaxing him. It still made no sense, but it mattered less.

"One more, and then we'll go," Kevin spoke as he stood up and went to the bar. He returned with two fresh pints.

They left the pub an hour and two more pints later, just after 1 p.m. Kevin walked with James to the carpark.

"Fuck. I'm over the limit. I can't drive."

Kevin laughed saying, "That's the spirit; losing your license is your biggest worry now. At least we have made some progress."

James burped, shook his head, and then smiled.

"I'm parked over by Churchill Square, drive carefully and park up at the beacon. I'll see you there."

"Ok," James concurred.

Even with the beer inside of him James felt that he was driving OK, he reflected on the 'practice' that he had had over the past few years. The driving was the easy bit; the pressure of five pints on his bladder was the real challenge. As he turned right onto Ditchling Road, the pain was so intense that it was the only thing he could think of. Two hundred metres on the right was a small lay-by, an entrance into the woodland behind. He pulled the car over, and jumped out with no consideration for his modesty, and started pissing by the door.

A car drove by, blasting the horn and yelling at him out of the window. He continued to pee.

"Man's second greatest pleasure," he muttered to himself.

He strode back to the car, the door wide open and the radio blasting. Another car pulled alongside of him and the driver got out.

"Great minds think alike," Kevin called over to him. "I'm becoming a bloody slave to my bladder."

He finished and then walked over to James in his car.

"OK, let's drive over to yours; I'll follow you."

The initial drive to the beacon is via a straight road on a gradual incline, with stunning views on both sides. Once the beacon is reached, the road descends, as if off a cliff, with a series of sharp bends on a narrow lane. It is a difficult road to navigate when sober, more so with five pints. Kevin, following James, was laughing out loud as the break lights signalled another sudden stop and the wing came within millimetres of the steep banks.

As the road levelled off, James made the sensible choice to drive into Ditchling and not go via Underhill Lane, where greater challenges would have awaited him.

Fifteen minutes later, with only one sudden stop for a pee ("once the seal is broken …," James called out) both cars pulled up outside of James' house. Sally was standing in the drive, she looked livid.

Sally came out of the shower, dried herself off, and walked down the stairs naked. She liked to surprise James, and it was his birthday. As she walked into the garden, she assured herself that there were no local neighbours and was excited at the thought of James' face as she walked towards him. Will he grab her and make love in the garden, or will they go indoors? The feel of the grass on her toes and the light breeze against her body made her feel like she should do this more often.

James wasn't in the garden; maybe he had gone upstairs and was waiting for her in the bedroom. Sally felt aroused as she walked up the stairs. She turned into the room and saw the bed empty. The thrill left her; the moment was gone. She pulled on her dressing gown and walked downstairs, expecting to see James in the kitchen. No sign.

As she walked into the living room and looked through the window, it was more the absence than the presence that she noticed. The car was gone. She walked to the door and opened it to confirm that the car was most certainly not there. Where had James gone?

She walked back into the house and considered the possibilities. None of it made sense, they had already agreed that she would drive him to the station to collect his car. It was only a few minutes' wait, what was the rush?

She went upstairs for her phone and sent a text message.

'Have you just driven off? What the fuck is happening, James?'

She waited for a response, but none came. She text again. And again. She tried to call him, two rings and then call declined.

The phrase, 'what the fuck?' has its time and place. This was the time and place. This was most unlike James. What the fuck?

Sally thought back to the earlier discussion and the mention of the MOT certificate. She recalled his sudden panic. Maybe there was more to the mileage than she imagined. She got dressed and went into the office. Where to start? She pulled out the file for MOT certificates and looked again. The four new trucks all showed a gradual increase in mileage, she made notes on a pad and each registered around 50,000 miles a year, give or take. DZ and SU around 1,000 miles. In fact, in one year, SU had registered just 633 miles.

She looked at the six files, one for each vehicle. The receipts were all crammed into a plastic folder, but she had photocopied each of them onto A4 paper for filling. Some sheets contained a single receipt, others five to the page - so much easier to review. She flicked through the receipts, trying to see something obvious, but could see nothing. She picked up a file for another vehicle, again, nothing obvious.

Pity Me.

It was the name of the service station that struck her, 'Pity Me'. A small village in Durham, the name evoked a previous catastrophe or maybe a corruption of the old Norman name 'Petite Mere'? The etymology wasn't what concerned her, it was the name that stood out. She looked at the receipt, 803 litres of diesel at £1.18 a litre, total cost £947.54. She went back to the folder for DZ and found a receipt for Pity Me, 803 litres of diesel at £1.18 a litre, total cost £947.54. The date on the receipt was different, in fact, it was two months later, but the cost and quantity were identical.

She loaded Numbers on her Mac and started a spreadsheet with the headings, 'location, number of litres, cost per litre, total'. She transcribed all of the receipts for DZ and then opened the file for AU, one of the new trucks. She went through each receipt and where there was a duplication, she added a tick to the added column 'AU'. Of the 35 receipts for DZ, 25 were duplicates of AU.

She added the missing entries for AU and then turned to the files for the other vehicles. The exercise took her nearly an hour. She looked at the results. A total of 203 receipts, of which 150 were duplicated at least once. She totalled up the duplication - almost £150,000.

She went through the other receipts for servicing, replacement tyres, overnight parking, oil, the list was endless, and so was the duplication. Over 80% of the receipts were duplicated at least once. Each had different dates, the registration number had changed, but the totals, the same. She looked at the non-duplicated invoices and found similarities, different service stations, different amounts per litre, different service items, but enough to suggest a careful copy and edit.

All told, there were over £400,000 in costs that were almost certainly faked.

She heard a car pull into the driveway, and then a second car. She went downstairs and opened the front door.

❖

Sally stood in the doorway, her face was serious. She looked James in the eye, his eyes moved away from her glance. He got out of the car and slammed the door, aware of her stare but trying his best to avoid it. As he walked towards her, attempting a smile, he heard Kevin slam his door and the crunch of the gravel under his feet.

"What the fuck is going on, James? And who the fuck is this?"

"This is Kevin, he is my, erm, partner."

Kevin walked towards Sally, his hand held out in greeting.

"A pleasure to meet you, Sally."

She ignored his hand and turned around, walking into the living room. James and Kevin followed her in.

"Sorry, quick pee," James rushed upstairs to the toilet, leaving Sally and Kevin standing in the living room. They both stared at each other as the sound of James peeing broke through the awkward silence. He farted and flushed the chain, running down the stairs.

"Kevin is my partner, I don't think you have met before?" James looked at Sally, his eyes pleading.

"No we haven't. Nor did I know you had a partner. I do your accounts, James and I have never heard of Kevin before. What the fuck is going on?" Sally's voice was going up and down, an attempt to control her anger and frustration.

All three took a seat as if by a silent instruction.

James started to talk, "Let me .."

Kevin raised his hand, a signal to James to stop talking.

"You've got a nice house here Sally, may I take a look around?"
Kevin started to stand up.

"Sit down," Sally asserted herself. No time for bullshitting.

Kevin sat down.

"I'm sorry. I was just trying to say, Sally, you have a nice house
here. You were living in a flat, where was it? In Landport? Yes, a
two bedroom flat in Landport estate just over three years ago. How
was that?"

Sally looked daggers at James as Kevin spoke. She was just about to
answer when Kevin started talking again.

"I can only imagine. Four of you in a two bedroom flat. James had
his own small haulage company, making a modest living. He didn't
need you to handle the books, then, did he? Turnover was less than
£200,000, after expenses and salaries, he made what? £20,000?
Maybe a bit more? So lucky that his business has improved and you
can live here. The kids? I assume that they are enjoying their
private schooling? I went to Winchester myself, private education
does give you that lift in life. Good for you in sending them away.
That's good parenting."

James had his head in his hands, Sally was sat open mouthed. So
many truths were uttered in such a sentence, why hadn't she thought
things through before?

Kevin stood up. "I think I will take a look around."

He didn't ask permission this time.

He walked into the kitchen where the custom built wooden units were painted a light green colour, the walls were white with a subtle shade of green. The Aga oven, turned off for the summer, in the corner, and a matching set of le Creuset pans hanging from hooks.

"Nice kitchen, not a factory job. Who did you use? I assume they were local?" Kevin called from the kitchen.

"Whitehorn," Sally's voice croaked. She wanted to scream at him to leave but could sense where the conversation was going.

"Mind if I pop upstairs?" It wasn't really a question; it was Kevin narrating where he was going next.

Sally and James sat in silence as they heard Kevin walking upstairs. They heard the creak of the floorboards.

"Really nice. You should be very proud of yourself, Sally, a perfect home to invite visitors. Any chance of a cup of tea? Earl Grey if possible."

Sally demurely stood up and walked to the kitchen.

"Sugar?" Her voice croaked again.

"Two please."

She walked back in carrying two cups, she didn't offer James one.

❖

Kevin sipped his tea in silence, Sally sipping hers in time with him. James sat with his head in his hands, wishing the moment would go away.

"Do you have much business experience, Sally?"

The sudden question shocked her as it broke the hushed sounds of sipping tea.

"I studied accounts to A level and I worked for a plumber in Brighton as an accountant."

"Good, so I don't need to explain the basics to you. Let's get straight to the point. As a rule of thumb, it costs a haulier around £1.50 a mile to run and pay for a truck, did you realise that they only do 8 mpg? That's around two miles per litre. This means a trip to Birmingham, say 200 miles, will cost £300. That's before we consider the salary of the driver, the cost to unload, and the return trip. Your average DIY factory in Newhaven would want to pay no more than, say, £2,000 to ship their goods to a warehouse in Birmingham and we are already pushing £900 in fixed costs. The haulage business is cutthroat, drivers from Eastern Europe offer their services a lot cheaper than your average Brit so we have to keep our costs low. If a truck is not running, it still costs us money in tax, lease payments, etc."

Sally looked at Kevin, nodding acknowledgment as he spoke, his crash course in the haulage business made sense, but why was he telling her this?

Kevin continued.

So, let's assume we have six trucks working five days a week, running 40,000 miles a year, that's £360,000 just in costs. We haven't paid the driver yet. We haven't paid any NI and pensions. We haven't paid the costs of the haulage yard. We haven't even paid James' salary. How do you think you can afford to pay your kids to attend private school? And two BMWs? You have expensive tastes, Sally. These things have to be paid for."

James had lifted his head from his hands, he hadn't expected Kevin to be so candid so quickly. He was doing all of the talking, and Sally seemed to be understanding. Maybe this won't be quite the problem he imagined?

"As a younger man, I used to look at my pay packet and ponder how rich I could be if I was to keep the tax and NI insurance I was paying. I could have afforded everything I wanted and it would be at no cost to anyone. OK the government misses out, but they are a bunch of crooks anyway. Just imagine how much we could make if we were to keep the costs?"

"You mean the diesel, service and other costs?" Sally was following the thread. She still had questions, but wanted to let him know she understood.

"Yes, those costs. Imagine how much richer we would be if we could keep the £360,000 I have just identified?"

"But, but these were costs, and we have to pay them. How do you intend to keep them?" Sally spoke and pondered.

Kevin was just about to answer when Sally answered her own question.

"Brunswick Haulage is just a shell? It doesn't deliver anything, does it?" She looked over to James. He had lied to her, no wonder he didn't want her visiting the yard. She thought of the times she had planned to drop in, but how he always told her not to bother as he had a dinner appointment with a client or how the yard was covered in an oil spill and was filthy. She never suspected a thing.

"Yes dear, it is just a shell."

As Kevin spoke, Sally glanced over at James who looked contrite. She glared at him, her anger was directed at his lying.

She turned her attention back to Kevin.

"But if it's just a shell, how does it make any money? It has to ship goods somewhere? It has to incur costs?"

Sally looked at Kevin for an response, he stayed silent, knowing she could work this out. She opened her mouth a couple of times to answer, closed it, and then opened again. Finally, she understood.

"So these costs come from a valid company? The four new lorries are real lorries and operate legally?"

"Yes dear. They do. In fact, if you look closely, you will find that these lorries, along with a few others, also operate from a few more yards around the South East. They are all registered under a holding company and 'loaned' to Brunswick and others. We hardly delivered a thing for over two years, yet we can charge the haulage and keep the costs," Kevin spoke with a charm in his voice, totally out of kilter with the information it was imparting.

Sally looked confused. At some point there needed to be a delivery somewhere to generate capital. Then it hit her.

"Money laundering?" The question was more of a statement. She knew the answer. Kevin nodded.

The game of 'join the dots' had begun, Sally had joined the first two dots the day before with the MOT certificates; she managed to join a few more as she went through the diesel receipts and even more as the service records became clear. She still couldn't see the picture, though, until she joined up the money laundering dot. With all of the dots connected she was looking at a grotesque image, one that included her house, her children's education, the cars in the driveway and the watch she bought James for his birthday. As she pondered this vision more, she realised that it included pretty much every luxury she had been able to enjoy over the past two years. Everything that had made her life more enjoyable and worthwhile was because of the money laundering dot. She retched and ran upstairs to the toilet.

Kevin looked over at James, "She's part of the plan now. She'll come about," he said looking around the room at the furnishings and fittings, "Once you achieve this, you never want to go back."

James started to relax, but only just. Sally finding out about the business was one thing, but he was in for a serious dressing down about the lies he had told her over the past years. One problem at a time, he thought as he attempted a smile.

Sally came back down the stairs, she looked determined. She, too, was smiling.

"James, it's 2 p.m. go make some lunch," Sally's order to James took him by surprise, firstly because of the mundanity of the task given the enormity of what she had just learned and, secondly, because he couldn't recall the last time he was expected to make any meal.

He pleaded with his eyes.

'Now, please, James, leave the men to talk."

James walked sheepishly into the kitchen.

"Right, to work. Please explain how this works, Kevin," Sally got straight to the point.

Kevin started, "I represent a client who has considerable funds, which, how can I put this? He would have difficulty demonstrating the providence of these funds and may be asked embarrassing questions."

"Your client is a crook, I get it. Move on," Sally had completed a number of online anti-money laundering courses as Company Secretary. She knew the source of funds was 'dirty' and had to be 'cleaned'.

"So he asks me to find companies from whom he can purchase services, in your case, transportation of goods. He pays the haulage fees, and you pay him via the lease you took out for the four new trucks. As simple as that."

"And, as the trucks don't actually exist, he pockets the full amount?"

"Almost correct. As I explained earlier, the trucks do exist. They are simply leased to many companies, and, in some cases, the lorries are used by these companies."

"In the same way that AU and DZ are used by Brunswick?"

"Yes, exactly," Kevin sipped his tea and smiled as he spoke the words.

"And the agency drivers?" Sally knew where this was going.

"My client also operates a driver agency."

"And the fuel receipts and services?" As Sally questioned the scheme she started to understand the simplicity of it.

"That is where I get my cut from. All of these receipts are, initially, genuine. I scan them in and make the changes necessary to customise them for your business, and you pay me."

"So we take the haulage fees, your client takes the agency and lease fees and you take the fuel and service costs?"

"Pretty much, simple eh?" He smiled as he spoke the words. He knew that Sally was now on-board, a catastrophe averted.

"Lunch," James called through from the kitchen. "Let's eat outside, shall we?"

James had knocked up a salad, this was the extent of his culinary skills. Throw in some lettuce, chop up the tomatoes and onion, boil a couple of eggs, and tip in a tin of salmon. He had found a few other 'salad looking' items in the fridge, which he washed, chopped or grated and dropped in the bowl. A bottle of something opportunely labelled 'salad dressing' later he had created his masterpiece.

Sally and Kevin had moved into the garden while James brought out the salad bowl and three small dishes. He went back inside and collected the bread, a bottle of water and some glasses. He eyes pleaded praise from Sally for preparing the food, none was forthcoming.

The meal was eaten with no reference to the haulage business, just trivial conversions on the weather, the plants in the garden and plans for a hen house next to the shed. Had any passersby looked on, they would be none the wiser as to the serious subject that had preceded this twee English gathering.

"James, please tidy away and wash up. I want to go through this in detail with Kevin," Sally said giving her instructions to her compliant husband.

She looked towards Kevin. "Let's go to my office and you can explain in more detail."

She stood up and Kevin followed her, she stopped at the foot of the stairs.

"Can you grab a chair, I've only got the one in my office. We are going to be some time."

Kevin collected one of the chairs from the dining table, a solid oak chair, and clumsily carried it up the stairs, following Sally.

He placed the chair down and watched as Sally brought up the spreadsheet and demonstrated her findings to Kevin.

"Well done, quite clever forensic work," he said, passing on his congratulations.

"Hardly," she sneered as she spoke the word, "this took me less than two hours. You need to be a bit more careful if we are to work together. This is shoddy and will send us all to prison."

Kevin smiled, she was definitely on board now.

"Maybe it would make sense to delete this document, it might be incriminating later on," Kevin made it clear that this was not a suggestion, this was an instruction.

Sally complied.

"Can we see where you have fucked up with your other records, please?" Sally opened the middle drawer of the filing cabinet and picked a file at random.

"Delivery of goods to Hawksley Enterprises, Skipsea, East Yorkshire. 16 pallets of goods, £20,000."

She opened up the browser and went to Google Maps, entering Skipsea. The map showed a small town on the east coast, north of Hull. She zoomed in, the town consisted of little more than a few roads, she flipped to the satellite image and saw a holiday camp and a series of bungalows along the coast. A road comes to a sudden end by the sea, the result of coastal erosion. Mr Moos Ice Cream Parlour was flagged. No obvious sign of industry. She looked at Kevin, he shrugged.

She right clicked the marker next to Skipsea and selected 'directions to here', Google maps returned a route of 270 miles. She opened the calculator and calculated 270 x 2 x 1.50.

"£810. That's quite a bit of profit margin on this one, not quite the tight margins you explained to me earlier?" As she spoke Kevin shrugged again.

She lifted the file to extract another invoice, the draught this created moved the invoice along the desk and it dropped behind. They both ignored it.

"Let's go through a few more. I need to understand how this works,

I'm the company secretary and I will need to defend this in an audit."

Kevin smiled again, she was well and truly on-board.

James sat in the living room, unsure what to do. He could hear Sally and Kevin talking, mostly Sally talking and Kevin offering monosyllabic responses to her comments. He wanted to join them but realised he wasn't welcome, Sally had made this clear. He thought about turning on the TV to watch the horse racing, but as he had not managed to place a bet, this seemed a fruitless exercise.

He tried to read the paper, but couldn't concentrate on the words, staring at a white sheet with occasional black markings. The tone from upstairs was civil, no raised voices, no anger, just the surreal sound of a normal business meeting. He looked at his watch; it was gone 4 p.m. They had been up there for nearly two hours.

The sound of a chair moving on the laminate floor and then the voice.

"Fuck me, my back is killing me, I need to stretch my legs," Kevin was exhausted sitting attentively on the hard dining room chair not designed for comfort over such a long period.

"OK, I think we have covered enough. Let's pop downstairs." Sally acknowledged both his physical plea and the implication that he had covered all he intended to.

Sally stood up and followed Kevin out of the small office and down the stairs.

James intuitively stood up, the junior partner showing respect as his seniors entered the room. He felt silly and sat down again.

"Cup of tea please, James," Sally barked her order to her compliant husband, he stood up again.

"No, please. Let me get it. You two have a lot of catching up to do," Kevin walked into the kitchen and James sat down again.

"Erm, how did it go?" James meekly asked Sally.

"Well Kevin has explained it all to me. Quite a tidy enterprise you have here, a few flaws but mostly tight. There's nothing that a bit of creative accounting can't overcome."

As Sally spoke she could see James noticeably relax.

"Oh, that's good. You can see why I went down this route. It's an easy way to make money, look at what this has bought us. With your accounting wizardry and my business acumen, we can do wonders. Maybe invest in some properties, a bit of divergence wouldn't do us any harm, would it?"

"You're just crooks. Fucking crooks. Kevin has kindly explained the process to me, I shall be heading to the police to explain the lot," the words were spat out in an angry tone, the sudden change shocked James.

Kevin could hear Sally's voice rise, and stuck his head around the door.

"Yes you. You fucking crooks. I would rather be living in a homeless shelter than this place because of its ill gotten gains. Don't look so surprised. Kevin here will be on the first plane to the Cayman Islands when the shit hits the fan, and we will be heading to prison. Judging by how quickly I unravelled it, this thing will fall apart in seconds if we're audited."

"Darling, .."

"Don't you fucking darling me, James. It's over. You've lied to me for three years. I thought you were a successful businessman, maybe even an ethical businessman. You read the Guardian for fuck's sake, always criticising me for my right-wing views. You're a fucking hypocrite. I want none of this. I just want to see you locked away. Goodbye James."

She stood up to leave, Kevin walked over, placed his hand on her shoulder, and pushed her down, gently at first but then more firmly as she resisted.

"Sit down!" Kevin shouted the words at her, spittle leaving his lips and splashing her top. She subconsciously wiped it with her hand.

"Do you realise the power that my client has? This house will be burned to the ground with you and your privileged children inside. You're just a small cog in a big machine. They would squash you with less thought than they might swat a fly, the words were strong enough, but the tone they were spoken in reeked of malice.

"Now listen to me, you cunt. You're going to do exactly as I say, otherwise, I will fucking ruin you and your weakling husband. You will be lucky if you reach prison alive, and, as I have people on the inside, luckier still if you survive a year once there," Kevin looked over at James who was shaking.

"Now James, your darling husband, will explain exactly how we are going to fix this, and fix it, we will. You will continue to live your privileged, cunty lifestyle and let your friends know how wonderful a businessman James is, and I will continue to collect my money.

36

Are we clear?"

Sally sat impassive, James nodded like the Churchill dog in the advert.

"So, it's two teas, no sugar, if I recall correctly?" Kevin didn't look for a response and returned to the kitchen.

"Darling. Look, we have to sort this out. You've heard Kevin, just come on board and everything will work out OK. Please."

James strung out the word 'please'. His eyes echoing the sentiment. He understood the danger they were in, he just wanted it to go away.

"I've told you, James, it's over. I'm off to report you now. Your threats are hollow; it's about time this scam was brought to an end."

Kevin could hear the conversation escalate, he knew that he couldn't turn Sally around, and unless he acted quickly, her threats would become real. There was a door off the kitchen that was slightly ajar. He pushed it and saw the utility room. In the corner was a golf bag. He grabbed a club and walked to the living room via the kitchen.

No words were spoken, he strode over to Sally, the golf club in his hand. He lifted the club, and with a single swing, he connected with Sally's ear. One second she was talking, her ire aimed at James, and the next she was silent.

A small drop of blood flowed from her ear.

"You've killed her?" James clearly spoke the words, hiding his obvious shock.

He repeated, "You've killed her?"

"No, she's not dead yet," Kevin held her wrist and could feel the pulse.

"We need to get an ambulance."

"No we don't, she will be dead soon enough. Hopefully she will last a few hours longer so we can get our story straight," Kevin said matter of factly

"You're shitting me, Kevin?" James looked at Kevin, unable to make sense of the last few seconds.

"No, I'm not. We need to work our way out of this." Kevin spoke so matter of factly, the simplicity of tight words sounded so sinister.

He looked at James and could see his reluctance.

"I can administer a similar knock to your head if you want?"

James turned white, he understood the threat was real.

"Do what I say and this will work out."

"How can you be sure? Sally saw through your books in a couple of hours."

"Let's just say, I am more skilled in some matters than I am accounting. I can use this club again before I put it down," Kevin reinforced the threat.

James nodded.

"Right, first thing. Grab a blanket or something to put over Sally. The blood will trickle and will end up on us. We don't need that."

As Kevin spoke, the small trickle of blood had dripped off her ear. He was impressed by his work, he knew the blow was fatal if left unattended, which it would be, but the lack of too much blood was really helpful.

James rushed upstairs, tipped the cushions off the bed, and grabbed the patterned quilt. He came back downstairs and looked to Kevin for direction.

"Put the fucking thing over her, do I need to tell you to do everything?"

James gently placed the cover over her head, letting it drape over her lap and down to her knees.

"OK, a murder weapon. We need a murder weapon," James looked at the club he was holding, confused why Kevin was asking such a question.

"No good, it's got my prints on. We need something else. Think man!"

James started to think. "Sally has played lacrosse since school. She stopped playing a couple of years ago, though, her sticks are in the loft."

"Well go get one, let me think the rest through."

James went upstairs. He reached to the loft and pushed it, no response. He pushed harder. He then noticed that where the ceiling was painted the paint has sealed the loft hatch. He went back downstairs.

"No joy; the hatch is sealed by paint. I could force it?"

"No, don't do that. It will look obvious. Let me think," Kevin stared into space while the cogs of his brain turned over.

"The accounts. Do you have any garden bags I can use?"

"Garden bags? Yes," James went into the kitchen and grabbed the roll of thick black bags. "How many?"

Kevin didn't answer, he walked up the stairs and signalled James to follow. He went into the office and opened the top drawer, flicking through the contents. All seemed to be personal. He closed this drawer and opened the middle one, the one that Sally had opened earlier. He grabbed a handful of the folders and signalled to James to open the bag. He dropped the folders in and repeated the process until the middle and bottom drawers were empty.

They walked down the stairs, Kevin was carrying four black bags loosely filled with the files.

"OK, I'm off to Brighton to buy a lacrosse stick. You will sit here and make sure that Sally doesn't come around. Don't try anything silly, I will find you. Sally stays here and dies and I will think this through. In the meantime, you are going to sit here and meditate. You have got to come back to your senses."

Kevin didn't wait for an answer. He picked up the golf club and walked out of the house. He clicked the car key and the lights flashed, he clicked again and the boot sprung open. He laid the golf club and garden bags in the boot and closed it. Thirty seconds later, he drove off.

James sat stationary, he closed his eyes so he couldn't see Sally. Her breathing had grown irregular, he tried to blank out the sound but couldn't.

❖

Meditation is a skill that is developed over years of practice, not something that just happens. It's the ability to clear your mind of all things and focus on just one, hopefully positive, thing. Sitting in the armchair opposite Sally, her shallow breathing muffled by the cover, did not represent the best way to achieve a positive outlook. The obvious thing to do would be to go into another room, but Sally would be there when he returned, so he had to focus on where he was sitting.

The negative thoughts came easily: Sally dying; the long prison sentence, ruined for life. These were the thoughts that he had to avoid. He closed his eyes and sat still, focused on his own breathing and imagining just how the fuck he was going to get out of this. For the second time in a few hours, he was reliant on Kevin coming up with a plan.

He completely ignored the fact that Kevin's initial plan had gone so wrong, and this was the reason they were struggling to fix the current situation.

James wasn't sure how long it was before he heard the car pull into the drive. He checked his watch, just before 7 p.m. He guessed that Kevin had been gone for around two hours. He stood up and walked to the door, looking over at Sally, her breathing sounded even more erratic.

"Is she dead yet?" The cold words from Kevin. James noticed that he was wearing driving gloves.

"I don't think so," James mumbled to himself as Kevin walked past him and, removing the gloves, checked her pulse.

"Another 10 minutes and she'll be gone," Kevin made his prediction to a confused looking James. He put the gloves back on.

"I told you, I have some experience in this area. Now if you don't want me to add you to my list of experiences, I suggest that you do exactly what I say."

The calm and measured tones for which Kevin was so renowned were still there, but now with an underlying menace. James nodded, he understood fully the threat and didn't doubt for one minute that Kevin would follow through.

"First things first, I need you to take the plastic cover off of this stick and place it outside the front door, I will put it in my car later."

As Kevin spoke, James obediently followed his words, he unwrapped the stick and walked to the front door, placing the plastic just outside.

"You do know this is a hockey stick and not a lacrosse stick, don't you?" James was unsure whether or not to point out such an obvious statement.

"You try buying a lacrosse stick in Brighton. I asked at two shops, and the staff hadn't even heard of it. Don't worry, hockey stick or lacrosse, it makes no difference. Right I want you to hold the stick, get a good grip, and swing it through the air a few times."

Kevin did as he was told.

"Now I going to lift the cover and I want you to rub the stick against Sally's ear and get a dab of the blood. Not too much, just a smudge."

As Kevin lifted the cover and Sally's face was exposed, James let out a yelp. Her face was ashen and damp. The colour had drained. The life had left her. Kevin was right, she didn't have much longer.

James closed his eyes as he gripped the stick and swung through the air. He re-opened them and carefully pressed the stick, at the point where it was curved, against the bloody ear. So carefully and gently, he didn't want to hurt his wife any more.

Kevin glanced around the room, his eyes stopped by the settee close to the window.

"Grab the stick by the tip and slide it under the settee, the blood side up. Just there. Leave around 2 inches of the stick showing."

James pushed the stick as instructed and felt it touch the wall behind, he then moved the tip to the left so that it was inserted diagonally, the last two inches on display.

"Right, now grab a tissue. I need you to have a quick J. Arthur."

"You want me to do what?" James knew exactly what he was saying, but was shocked at the suggestion.

"Rub one off. It's your birthday, and Sally would have treated you today."

Suddenly the magnitude of what Kevin was asking him came to the fore.

"You're stitching me up for Sally's murder? You have got to be kidding?"

"As I say, you have two choices. You leave here in handcuffs, or you leave here in a body bag. Your choice. And I know you won't say anything, I have a lot of friends on the inside, you won't last two minutes unless you do what I say. And don't worry, I have a plan to get you off. Trust me on this."

James stood open mouthed; the menace was real. The plan to get him off? What was this?

"Now pop along, the computer is upstairs. A few minutes of what does it for you, and then bring the tissue back down, please. I see you're hard already, quite common in these circumstances," he pointed to his own groin, "shouldn't take you too long."

James walked up the stairs, was he really going to wank on command? Two minutes later, he appeared on the stairs again.

"See, I told you it wouldn't be an issue. Right, we need to get this into Sally's pants," he lifted the cover again and then hesitated.

"It's not going to work, too much blood. I'm going to tilt her forward, you run the tissue along her arse crack, pretend she gave you a brown pass, eh?"

James followed obediently, he had no idea what he was doing or why, and even less so what a brown pass was.

Kevin moved her back, Sally took her last breath. They both looked at each other in silence.

Sally's phone rang.

They looked at the phone ringing; it had gone unnoticed until then. Sally's phone was resting on the small table by her chair.

"Answer it man," Kevin was growing frustrated at the continuous ringing. James moved forward, picked up the phone, and pressed answer.

"Uh, hello. This is James"

"Hello, is Sally Gordon there, please?"

"No, Sally is not around at the moment," James stared at Sally's lifeless body, "Can I help?"

"Sure, Sally ordered a takeaway for 7 p.m., did she forget?"

James subconsciously looked at his watch, it was 7.15 p.m. Of course, Sally said she had ordered them a takeaway for his birthday.

"Of course, she must have forgotten. I will come over and collect it. What is the address?"

The caller provided the details.

"Thank you. I should be there in 10 minutes," he hung up the call.

"Sounds like we will be able to have something to eat," Kevin smiled. "What's the address, I will go and collect it. Be a good boy and lay the table."

Kevin left the house to collect the food. He didn't notice that the plastic covering that had wrapped the hockey stick had blown under the bush by the front door.

Fifteen minutes later, Kevin returned with the plastic bag, which he passed it to James.

"Be a good chap and dish us up dinner. I'm going to explain how we are going to get out of this mess."

The food was either excellent or both of them were starving, they both ate as though this was their last meal. James started to think it might well be.

Kevin spoke clearly, and James listened. By the end of the meal, James felt a lot happier. Kevin was a clever man.

James stood up to put the plates into the dishwasher, and Kevin held onto the knife, fork, and wine glass and walked to the sink, washing them carefully and placing them on the drainer.

"Phone," Kevin gestured.

James passed him the phone, Kevin tried to navigate the apps, but his driving gloves made this impossible. He passed the phone back to James.

"Go into your text messages and delete the messages you sent me today, and remove me as a contact,"

James obeyed and showed the evidence to Kevin, who acknowledged.

"What about your phone?" James knew that deleting the texts and contact details was one thing, but the phone number was still tied to a phone and could be traced.

"I removed the SIM when we left the Druids and placed the phone in a bin. I suspect it is headed for the incinerator already," Kevin said, making it clear just how well thought-out this plan was.

Kevin then went upstairs to the office, where he had sat with Sally earlier. He carefully wiped the surface of the desk and the drawers (in particular the backs of the handles where his fingers would have touched). He went into the kitchen, his memory recalling all of the places he may have touched.

James watched on, this clearly wasn't the first time he had tried to remove his presence.

"Now do exactly as I say. Don't deviate, and this will all work out ok?"

James looked as Kevin spoke, he agreed - all would be OK.

Chapter Three

He had made the phone call from his mobile four minutes ago, just after midnight. He didn't want to make the call any earlier as it would have spoiled his birthday.

"This is Detective Thomas, how can I help you?"

"Detective, I have just killed my wife Sally, I think you should come over."

"Pardon, could you say that again, please," although Chris had heard the words quite clearly, he wanted to be sure.

"Detective Thomas, I have killed my wife. Sally is sat on the armchair in front of me, very dead. Can you come to my house in Offham, near Lewes."

James then went on to confirm his address.

James checked his watch, another 6 minutes had passed with no sound of a car approaching. He remained seated. Should he go to the toilet? It had been a couple of hours since he last went for a pee. It wouldn't be a wasted trip, but he didn't feel that he needed to go.

He hadn't had a drink during that time. He thought back to the last one, a cup of instant coffee nearly three hours ago. He had contemplated making a fresh pot of filter but wasn't sure he would be able to finish the full pot in time, it seemed such a waste. As he made the coffee, having to break up the solid block of hardened granules, he realised that he hadn't drank instant for a long time. He had a single sip, it tasted bitter. He sipped a few more times, hoping it might improve, but it didn't.

He stared now at the mostly full cup by his side; it must be stone cold by now.

The clock on the wall showed the time as 19 minutes past midnight, his phone showed 23 minutes past. He had more faith in the phone as he understood this was synchronised wirelessly from an atomic clock. He pondered how long the wall clock had been wrong. Should he reset it now, or leave it? He felt himself lifting off of his chair, OCD always wins, just as he heard the sound of a car in the distance. He waited a few more seconds and then saw the reflection of the blue light at the edge of the curtains.

James stood up, preempting the knock, and started to walk to the door. He turned towards the curtains and straightened the ruffle behind the sofa, allowing them to hang straight. He was a few metres from the door when there was a knock, the preceding silence had disappeared. When would he experience the joy of silence like that again?

"Mr Gordon? Please could you open the door."

The gap between the knock and DC Chris Thomas talking lasted less than a second. He had seen the light from the living room and noticed what he thought was a twitch from behind the curtains.

The door opened, "Detective Thomas?"

James spoke clearly, no sign of the nervousness that most would feel knowing that they would be facing many years in jail.

"Mr Gordon, please could you step outside."

Chris pointed to the uniformed men who stood behind him. James saw the gesture and started to walk in the direction of the constable, who was holding cufflinks in his right hand. He held out both hands in submission as the rings were tightened around his wrists.

"Would I be able to collect a few things detective?" James' attention was directed to Chris. He was making it clear that the uniformed presence was just wallpaper.

Chris started to answer just as the constable asserted his presence. "Let's get you down the station. If you need anything, let me know we can send someone to collect, if appropriate."

"Maybe a coat?" James tried to make the request not seem like a plea.

The constable looked at the still sky and felt the relative warmth of the summer night, "I should think you'll be OK without a coat, sir, I can't imagine you will need to be going outside for some time." He smiled at the implication of time, he meant a few days, but knew that James would hear this as prison time.

James turned and looked at his house, sighed, and then walked to the car and got in the backseat, helped by the constable, who gently pressed his crown to make sure he didn't bang his head as he got in. The door was slammed.

The second constable was already unloading equipment from the boot of the car and had started to tape off the drive way with a long strip that read, "Police - Do not pass."

"If you can wait there, I will just have a quick look around," Chris spoke to the back of the uniformed policeman who offered no resistance to the suggestion, they had seen their share of dead bodies and felt sure they would sleep better later if denied the opportunity of seeing another one just now.

Chris walked into the living room, slipping on a pair of latex gloves, and immediately saw the body in the armchair. Careful not to disturb anything, he gingerly walked towards it and lifted the blanket. Her face was ashen, the pupils of her eyes cloudy, she certainly looked dead. He looked down at her wrist as he lifted it, the skin was cold and clammy, the blood had drained from the top of the wrist and settled at the base. He didn't feel that he didn't need to check her pulse, she was definitely dead, but procedures required that he confirm her death, and the absence of a pulse was one of them. He gripped her wrist and subconsciously looked towards his watch as if to measure her heart rate. He felt no pulse.

He looked around the living room, nothing else appeared untoward. Ever aware of contaminating a murder scene, he checked the other rooms downstairs, which were all empty. He walked up the stairs, it was a large house, so he suspected four rooms. A quick count on the landing showed him five doors, four bedrooms and a bathroom? One door was opened, and he pushed it gently, the master bedroom he assumed.

He checked the other rooms in turn, just for a quick look. Two of the rooms were children's rooms, both empty. The beds were neatly made and the rooms tidy, if a child has used them recently, they wouldn't be so tidy. A third room was setup as an office space, with a desk with a large iMac taking pride of place and a few sparse shelves against one wall.

He walked back down the stairs and outside, removing the latex gloves as he walked.

"There is a dead body, but no one else is inside," Chris directed this to the constable, who took this as an unspoken instruction.

51

The constable picked up the radio and started to talk, "This is Sierra Alpha One Three, attending premises in Offham with suspected 187. Please can you send support and forensics."

"Copied Sierra Alpha One Three, will send support and forensics over."

The dispatcher responded calmly, belying the chaos that was just about to ensue back at the station. Murder is, fortunately, not that common an occurrence, but once the trigger has been pressed and one is announced, the police have to act quickly.

Chris opened the door and looked at James for only the second time.

"You will be taken to the police station shortly. Before you leave, I notice that there are two children's bedrooms. Are they with friends tonight?"

"Detective Thomas," he insisted on addressing Chris directly, "my two daughters are at their boarding school, they are not scheduled to be home for a couple of weeks."

"OK," he looked at the constable, "Dave, can you ensure that family support team take details and send someone out to the children?"

"Will do," he nodded at Chris and turned towards James in the back of the police car as he closed the door for a second time, "Let's be getting you down the station." He started the car. Dave's colleague, Eric, tapped the roof of the police car, and Dave drove off.

Eric continued taping off the scene and then stood by the entrance for the long night ahead, he looked at the cloudless sky and felt the warm air, 'at least it'll be a warm one', he thought to himself.

❖

Chris watched as the police car left, the blue lights flashing, but the siren turned off in respect of the time of night. The white Mercedes was parked in the driveway, it was close to a full moon, so the car was lit up. It had been cleaned recently, the windscreen was mostly clear with just a few flattened insects, and the bodywork was gleaming under the moonlight. He placed his hand on the bonnet. It was cold. He tested the exhaust pipe, cold again. No one taught him this during the detective training, he had gleaned it from the numerous TV shows on crime. He assumed, from his very unscientific way of testing, that the car hadn't been driven for a couple of hours.

Chris strode over to the back of his car, a three year old Ford Focus,120,000 miles on the clock and bodywork that told the tale of every one of those miles. The police had a limited pool of cars, and these were driven around the clock as shifts changed. He opened the hatchback, found and unwrapped a fresh white coverall, removed his jacket and stepped into the coverall, zipping it up to his chin. He grabbed the small torch and placed it in his pocket.

"Eric?" Chris called to the constable, who was busy securing the scene with the 'Police - Do not cross' tape, "I'm just popping indoors. I shouldn't be too long."

Eric nodded.

As he walked towards the door of the house, he looked back at the Focus and turned around, leaning into the driver's side, and put the hazard lights on. If nothing else, this would at least highlight the location to the drivers that he was expecting very soon. He walked towards the house again.

Standing just inside the door, placing plastic overshoes over his feet and then put on a fresh pair of latex gloves. Treading carefully and trying not to move anything, he repeated his look around the house. Forensics will be here shortly, he thought, but he wanted the first look. As he walked into the living area, he stared again at the dead body, assuming this was James' wife, but until this was proven, he didn't want to give the body a name. If he was American, he would be calling her Jane Doe, but he rejected most Americanisms.

Looking around the room, he tried to take in the scene. The body was sitting upright in the armchair, upright, her head leaning forward. It was wrapped in a thin duvet cover, he looked closer and suspected it was possibly a decorative cover for the bed, the type of thing that is thrown on the floor, along with the numerous cushions and stuffed animals that are common place on beds, to allow enough space to get into the bed. A large bloodstain was present at the head level and ran down the cover, not quite reaching the carpet. He suspected (wrongly) that she had been covered by the blanket and hit with something solid; the absence of any obvious blood splatter suggested that the covering had prevented this.

On the other side of the room, opposite the chair, was another armchair. The cushions were moved to one side and crumpled, the rest of the room was so neat that this small untidiness stood out. This must be where James was sitting. On the floor to the right of the chair was a cup of black coffee, three quarters full. Chris held his hand close to the cup, no heat was radiated. He was careful not to touch the cup but felt confident the contents were cold.

What about a murder weapon? He looked around the room for something that might be used, everything looked in place. The fireplace had a combination set, but everything looked brand new apart from the small shovel, which had traces of ash. The wood burning stove was spotlessly clean and served as a decoration during the summer months. The logs were neatly stacked either side of the stove, none had any obvious bloodstains, and the way the logs were stacked symmetrically suggested that none had been removed.

The clock showed the time as 45 minutes past midnight, he double checked his watch to confirm this was showing the right time. It was close enough.

Another quick glance around the living room, everything looking in place, it reminded him of the numerous apartments that he had recently viewed in Brighton, all spotlessly clean as a result of a last minute tidy-up, in his so far, failed attempt to find a suitable place to purchase with his DC's salary. The curtains hung straight, the cushions on the settee must have been shaken and puffed out, and even the remote controls for the TV, DVD, Apple TV, etc. were lined up in a neat row by the TV on the spotlessly clean glass surface.

A picture of Sally and James was in pride of place on the window ledge. It looked pretty recent, in that the image of James looked close to the man he had just sent off to the police station. He took out his phone and took a quick photo, which might come in handy for future questions with witnesses.

Chris walked towards the kitchen, passing the body in the armchair. In the corner of his eye he caught something. He turned quickly to see what it was and looked around again. He was convinced that he had seen something, it took a further scan of the room before he caught the edge of the object sticking out from under the settee.

He leaned down to try and make it out, moving nothing. He instinctively went to use the torch app on his phone, but as his latex clad hands touched the glass front he recalled the futility of trying to use the touch screen while wearing gloves. Instead, he used the small pen torch he carried in his pocket.

The beam was pointed at the object, highlighting what must be a handle but not revealing much more. The skirt along the bottom of the settee sat neatly along the carpet and prevented any further inspection. Cricket bat? Rounders bat? A tennis racket? He looked closer, the way it seemed to lay flat against the carpet suggested a flat, not round, surface.

"Methinks a hockey stick," Chris muttered to no one but himself.

Standing up, he moved towards the kitchen. Spotless, not even a cup in the sink, the cupboards all closed and the sides wiped. The door to the dishwasher was closed; he suspected that this too would be empty but didn't check.

An internal door seemed to go to another room, he guessed a utility room but was determined not to open in case it disturbed the scene further. He backed out of the kitchen and headed back into the living room.

Chris walked up the stairs again, the bedroom doors slightly ajar as a result of his initial check. Just as he stuck his head in the door of one of the rooms, he heard the sound of another car approaching, expecting it to pass but it slowed down and came to a halt outside the house.

His watch said 00.47. "Fuck me, that was quick." Chris wasn't expecting anyone to turn up that quickly, must be a record. He headed back down the stairs.

❖

"Hi Abi, I thought you had a job over in Hove?" He spoke to the female detective as she opened the car door.

Abi, like Chris, was still in her first year as a detective and still a year away from her 25th birthday. Both were graduate recruits who had chosen not to take the fast track route offered to graduates, preferring to do their time the hard way.

"Just a break in. The guy was securing his window as I arrived and felt confident the insurance would cover. I had a quick look around, nothing was stolen as they were interrupted and ran. He's going to pop into the office tomorrow to complete the paperwork. Sounds like you have pulled a good one?" Abi was keen to get involved in this case, for both, this was their first murder. This was the stuff they had trained for.

"The suspect is called James Gordon, he phoned in to report he had killed his wife. She's inside if you want to take a look?"

"OK, let's go see Jane Doe then," Chris grimaced at her, she knew he hated Americanisms and taunted him with them all the time.

"Coveralls," Chris called to her as she walked to the door. His signal made her turn tail and go back to the car. Abi donned the same outfit as Chris, carrying her shoe covers and fitting them as they reached the door.

"It looks pretty straight forward. Sally Gordon, let's assume Mr Gordon provided the correct information, is covered with a bed quilt, there is no pulse. Mr Gordon was sat patiently waiting for my arrival, I assume he was sitting in this chair as the seat was still warm when I arrived. TV turned off and no music. Her skin was clammy when I tested the pulse, I suspect she has been dead for some time. He must have sat there all this time just looking at her."

Abi looked around the room as he spoke, trying to take in the situation. "How do you think she was killed? Have you found a weapon?"

'Just under the settee there, there seems to be something sticking out."

"A hockey stick," Abi was quick to recognise it, "looks like an Grays GR7000 to me."

Chris looked puzzled, how on earth could she work out the brand and model from the short bit of wood sticking out.

"I played all the way through school and still play the odd game now," she said, spotting his confusion.

He nodded, but wasn't overly sure.

"It's top of the range, she obviously played a lot."

Chris looked around the room as he spoke. "Maybe she played a lot? Maybe she simply bought the best because she had the money? It doesn't look as though they were short of a bob or two?"

"Ok, we can check. What else have you found out?"

Chris was just about to respond when they heard another car draw up. "Sounds like forensics have arrived. It's best we pop outside and let them take over."

Abi nodded approval.

Both walked outside as two people were exiting their car.

"Greetings. This must be your first one?"

They both acknowledged.

"Well I hope you haven't touched anything inside," Benjamin knew as he asked the question that the two had a reputation for following the regulations to the letter.

"Of course they haven't," Billie confirmed what he was already thinking. "Give them a break; this is their big moment."

Billie and Benjamin, also known as 'Bill and Ben' much to their chagrin, were the forensic team.

"Ok, just kidding you guys. Let's see what you've got."

Abi looked over at Chris, a silent signal for him to take the lead and talk. He then started to explain in detail what he had seen.

"Very thorough summary," Billie sounded pleased, "I guess you'll be heading to the station to interview the suspect? Or will one of you be staying with us?"

Both were keen to stay; they both suspected a treasure-trove of forensic evidence in the house. This time, Chris looked at Abi and shared the silent signal.

"Yes, I'll stay with you. Chris will head to the station"

"Off you go, Chris," Billie jokingly pushed Chris to one side, smiling as she did it. "Let's leave this to the professionals."

"Speak later." As he walked to the car he removed his gloves and coveralls. Bill and Ben started to put on theirs, gathering their equipment as they walked into the house.

"At least it's a nice night for it, Eric?" Chris looked at the cloudless sky and felt the warmth in the air.

"Well it beats hanging around West Street, that's for sure. Dave just radioed through to say Mr Gordon is tucked up in his cell for the night."

"Well, let's go wake him up then," Chris looked again at the night sky, "he's not going to be able to enjoy an evening like this for some time is he?"

Chapter Four

Abi was passed the video camera and told to follow Bill and Ben's guide as they went around the house, trying to catalogue everything.

Billie looked at the analogue clock on the wall, the small hand was a couple of minutes before the three quarter mark. She checked her watch to be sure. It was four minutes out.

"The time is 01.47, we are at the premises of James Gordon and his wife, Sally Gordon. He called 999 shortly after midnight, claiming to have killed Sally."

The camera was facing Sally's body as Billie spoke, Abi was assured that the microphone would pick up their voices but was extremely keen to ensure it moved in Billie's direction as she spoke.

"The body is covered by what looks like a Laura Ashley design quilt. There is a large blood stain starting from the head and running down to the end of the quilt cover."

As Billie spoke, a drop of blood fell from the quilt and hit the carpet, as if it had progressed slowly along the length of the quilt and waited for that moment to reach the tip. No sound was made as it reached the carpet, but the blood splashed as it hit, creating a stain about the size of a 5p coin. Each of them had noticed the drip and stood silently awaiting a second drop. A few seconds later, the second drop appeared. They imagined the thud as it hit the carpet.

Billie held Sally's wrist and continued her monologue.

"No sign of a pulse, the skin is cold and suggests she died some time ago," she held one of the fingers and tried to move it, it was stiff and didn't try to force it. "Rigor mortis has set into the fingers, looks like she has been dead for at least 3-4 hours. We will get confirmation of the time of the death shortly."

As Billie spoke, Benjamin was taking pictures of the body in situ, and he signalled to her that he had the scene covered. Billie lifted the bottom of the blanket to expose the legs. Sally was wearing a patterned dress that came down just below her knees; her legs were bare beneath the knee, and was wearing no shoes. Her lower calves and feet were purple where the blood had settled.

"The blood has settled in her lower limbs, I would hazard a guess that she has been dead for at least 4 hours, possibly longer. What time did he call the police?"

"Just after midnight," Abi said, conscious that her mouth was close to the microphone on the camera. She spoke quietly, more of a whisper.

"You don't need to be too quiet, Abi, we're not filming a Hollywood epic here. Just enough to capture the scene."

"Just after midnight," she repeated the words again, a bit louder.

"He must have been sitting here with her for two or three hours before he called, I think," Billie spoke the sentence as a question.

"Nod," Benjamin acknowledged the question.

Billie lifted the quilt slowly as Benjamin continued to take pictures, the digital camera making the mechanical whirr artificially added by the manufacturers to create the authentic sound of an older analogue device. As she lifted the cover, it started to lift the dress, the blood sticking the two fabrics together. She placed a finger in the dress and continued to lift the quilt, the two fabrics silently separating.

Slowly, the body was exposed, the blood stain running along her left-hand side the right of her body seemingly blood free. The quilt had soaked up the trickle of blood as it obeyed the laws of gravity and flowed to the floor.

As the cover was lifted higher, it started to grip the dress more, the blood forming a bond with the quilt cover. Bille held the dress tightly and felt the drag as the coagulated fluid gave way.

"Here goes," Billie said.

No matter how many murders the police attend throughout their career, the sight of the mortal wounds will always shock. As they had followed the blood along the body from the ankles upward, they knew what to expect and that it wouldn't be a pretty sight. Slowly, Sally's head came into view, Abi had moved around as the cover was lifted to ensure this moment was captured. She gasped as the head was exposed.

The custody suite is located in the Hollingbury estate, just across from the large Asda superstore, a modern structure bookended by 1960s architecture. Concrete designs with subtle curves to try and improve the ugliness of the edifice. Designs that made sense in the drug-fueled sixties, the impact of an evening on marijuana, and the resultant couldn't care less attitude. The custody block, in comparison, was a plain box building with added cladding and would have benefited from the architects having a couple of tokes.

Chris drove up to the entrance and pressed the buzzer. A small camera captured his car, he was attempting to lift his ID card to the camera, but the security guard recognised the car and Chris as he had visited many times before, so much for procedure. The large metal gates opened, and he drove through and parked the car. The time was just after 2 a.m, he had been on duty since 6 p.m. but wasn't feeling tired. The adrenaline was rushing through his veins, the excitement of his first murder investigation.

He walked to the main entrance and pressed the buzzer, a few seconds later and the click of the security guard pressing the microphone.

"Detective Constable Thomas," he looked at the small camera.

"Can I see your ID, please?"

Chris sighed and reached into his pocket, took out the ID, and pressed it to the camera. The door clicked, and he pushed it open.

Oli stood waiting as he arrived, his head beckoning to the suited gentleman seated behind him. Chris's face looked puzzled.

"It's Mr. Gordon's solicitor. He was here when we arrived?"

"Wow, that was quick. Did he call from the car or something?". Chris stared at the gentleman, acknowledging his presence.

"Nope, he was here when we arrived. Gordon must have spoken to him before he called us. A lucky guess that he would be taken here, I suppose?"

Before Chris could reply the solicitor stood up, straightened his suit, adjusted his tie and walked towards them both.

"Charles Beadle," he said, holding out his hand as he approached. Chris reciprocated, offering his hand. Charles grabbed his hand in tight grip and moved to the side, twisting his wrist and forcing Chris's palm to face up, a controlling gesture.

"I assume you will want some time with your client before we begin?" Chris assumed, correctly, that there had been no opportunity for Gordon to meet his solicitor and welcomed the opportunity to leave them alone for a few minutes while he grabbed a cup of coffee.

"No, that shouldn't be necessary. Shall we get straight down to business?"

Sally had been clearly hit with something solid on the left side of her head, it looked like a single violent blow, but no one could be sure at this stage. Ben continued taking pictures, moving about to get a clear view from all angles.

"Looks like a single blow with something hard, did you find any candidates when you were looking around Abi?"

Abi looked towards the settee and saw the handle of the hockey stick protruding. "There is a hockey stick there."

"Hockey? Can you be sure?" Bill seemed surprised that this could be identified from only a couple of inches.

"I still play the odd game, used to play a lot at school, it looks like Grays," Abi felt she was repeating herself and expected that she would be explaining the rules of the game a few more times during this investigation.

"Well, let's take a look then. Can you grab a bag Abi?" Bill walked over to the settee, waiting for Ben to capture the end of the stick. Using two fingers on the tip, she slowly pulled the stick out and held it up for a short investigation.

"It looks new, possibly unused. And it is a Grays," Bill looked to Abi, offering praise.

Abi leaned closer to look at the stick. "I would go so far to say it is brand new, never been used. The shaft has never been taped, and there are no dents."

Bill leaned and turned the stick to get a view from different angles. "Well, I can see a small smudge of blood, so this looks like a candidate." She started to put it in the bag that Ben was holding when Abi interrupted her.

"Can I take a closer look?"

Bill held the stick and started to turn as if by untold instruction. Abi looked up and down the shaft as it was turned for over a minute.

"OK, I'm done," Abi stepped back and gave the signal to bag the item.

"Something strange?" Bill looked at Abi who was looking puzzled.

Abi didn't respond immediately.

"I'm not sure, it doesn't seem right. The stick is obviously brand new, and the shaft is still untaped. I've used a few new sticks in my time, and you can see the damage that a single game will do. There's no real difference between 'hardly used' and 'used' when it comes to these sticks."

"I'm not sure of your point, this is a new stick and it has never been used. I get that, what else is on your mind?" Bill could detect that the rookie detective had seen something and wanted to encourage her to open up.

"What I am saying is that these sticks bruise easily. It would take quite some force to hit and kill someone with a single blow, yet the stick looks fresh."

"It depends where the person has been hit," Ben opined, "the area of the skull by the ear is the weakest, and it wouldn't necessarily require that much force to make a fatal blow," he looked to Bill for confirmation.

"Maybe," Bill said, stringing out every letter of the word.

"OK, let's not draw any conclusions just yet. Let's see if there are any other options."

As a millennial, Chris had never come across cassette tapes growing up. His dad was a keen collector of music and had shelves for CDs and vinyl, but no cassettes. He still recalled the laughter during training when the interview process was described and two cassette tapes were unwrapped and placed in the machine. All of the probationers studied the tapes with interest, and when told that the 90 in C90 stood for minutes, they were shocked by the small capacity for such a large item.

He was aware of the trials for digital recording by some police forces, but, as he unwrapped two fresh cassettes, he knew that they would be reliant on this old technology for some time to come.

Chris instinctively looked at his watch, before glancing at the clock on the wall. He pressed the record button on the tape machine, and both cassettes started to turn.

"The time is 2.55 a.m. on Sunday 28th June. Present are James Gordon, his solicitor, Charles Beadle, and myself, Detective Constable Chris Thomas. Before I start, I need to read you your rights, Mr. Gordon."

"You do not have to say anything, but, it may harm your defence if you do not mention when questioned something which you later rely on in court. Anything you do say may be given in evidence. Are you happy for the interview to begin?"

James looked over at Charles for confirmation before replying.

"Yes, please proceed."

"James Gordon, you contacted 999 this morning at," Chris checked his notes, "six minutes past midnight. The call was transferred to me, and your words at the time were,"

Again Chris checked the notes, he was sure that they were recorded verbose but recordings would back these up.

"'Detective, I have just killed my wife Sally, I think you should come over.' And you then confirmed, 'Detective Thomas, I have killed my wife. Sally is sat on the armchair in front of me, very dead. Can you come to my house in Offham, near Lewes'. Can you confirm that these were the words you used when calling the police?"

"Of course I can't confirm these words, I wasn't taking notes like you were, but this was certainly the gist of what I was saying,"

68

James spoke with a cocky confidence that surprised Chris.

James looked Chris in the eye as he spoke and held his gaze as if he were going to say more.

Chris was taken aback by his directness. Whereas he had sought his solicitor's confirmation before replying to the opening statement, in response to this question, his answer was immediate and didn't require support.

"So. to confirm, you are admitting to the murder of Sally Gordon?"

"Detective, my client said nothing about murder," Charles jumped in promptly.

"Sorry, I will repeat my question. You are admitting that you killed your wife, Sally Gordon?"

"Again, detective. My client has not admitted to killing his wife."

Chris looked dumbfounded at the statement and was just about to ask a fresh question when Charles clarified.

"My client has merely confirmed his statement when he called you earlier on."

The clarification did nothing of the sort as far as Chris was concerned. He decided to rephrase the question, but before he could ask again, the solicitor spoke.

"Detective. I would like to take some time to speak to my client. Can we stop the interview now, please?" Charles took great pleasure in Chris's confusion and relished the control this gave him.

"The time is 2.58 a.m. The interview is ended."

Chris pressed the button on the tape machine and signalled for the assistant to come in.

"Please can you escort Mr. Gordon back to his cell."

Chris then turned to the solicitor, "We will make the arrangements for you to see your client. Please, take a seat outside, and we will let you know when he is ready."

Two people can play these games, he thought.

Charles accepted Chris's play. Pointless arguing, he thought. He stood up and walked outside as James was escorted back to his cell.

"Can you call the boss?" The receptionist called over to Chris.

"What now?" Chris looked at his watch. Surely the boss was asleep?

"Yes, he called 5 minutes ago," the receptionist confirmed

DI Tom Christopher, aka the boss, seemed to be aware of new cases as they came up.

Chris picked up his phone, selected the Detective Inspector from his favourites, and hit dial. The call was answered before the first ring.

"I hear you've got your first big one?" Chris was starting to wilt, yet his boss sounded wide awake.

"You're awake? I would have called if I had known."

"Don't worry yourself; as you get older, it's not so easy to sleep all night, and I called the desk to keep an eye on you. Is Abi with you?" Tom started to take control.

"Abi is at the house with forensics. I was planning to call her. I'm glad you've called, though; I have had the strangest of interviews," he went on to explain what had happened.

"What time do you knock off?"

"6 a.m., I am back to days tomorrow so will be in the office for 3 p.m." Chris confirmed his schedule.

"OK. Head back to the office and write up what you have so far, and I will take over when I get in."

"Any chance I can come in early, I don't want to miss out on this one," Chris' enthusiasm shone through.

"I thought you might ask that. OK, but no earlier than midday. Go back and write up your notes now. I'll call Abi shortly." Tom was firm in his response.

Abi continued to record the session as the forensics team moved about the place, making mental notes to follow up on later. It had been nearly two hours, and they had still not left the living room.

"I think we can move the body now," Bill said.

Abi seemed relieved, the camera she was using was only a palm sized device, but so determined to capture everything, she had exaggerated the hold and felt quite stiff as she lowered it.

All three of them moved outside of the house, removing their face coverings and latex gloves. Bill took her phone out of her pocket and dialled the mortuary to arrange a pickup. Ben walked towards the 'Police - do not cross' tape, took the tin from his pocket, opened it and started to roll a cigarette. He offered the tin to Eric who was standing patiently by the driveway.

"Don't mind if I do," Eric acknowledged the offer, pinching the tobacco and rolling to create a thick rollie. Prior to joining the police, he had served 10 years as a prison officer. The prisoners only had access to limited tobacco and rolled the thinnest tube, carefully preserving the scarce resource. His cruel response was to roll the thickest, a habit he retained to this day even though he had 'given up' for months.

Ben lit his and offered the lighter to Eric. They both drew in the smoke in silence and contemplated the still morning and the glow from the east as the sun started to rise and reflect on the few clouds.

Abi looked at her phone, a text message from Chris, 'call me when you can', She looked at the time, it was 3.55 a.m.

"Whats up Chris?" Chris answered the phone as soon as it rang, clearly, the interview had ended.

"We've got a strange one," he went on to explain the interview, almost verbatim as it was so short.

"The boss called as soon as I got out of the interview."

"That's early even for him," Abi said, sounding surprised.

"He never sleeps, we should know by now. For someone counting down his retirement, he remains pretty keen."

"Yeah, so what did he say?"

"He's taking over when he gets in, and probably on his way now. He asked me to come in early," Tom hadn't actually asked and it wasn't Chris's intention to suggest otherwise, so he didn't correct himself.

"What time, I'll join you?" Abi was as keen as Chris to remain on the job.

"I can't say he will complain. I'm just finishing off my notes now and will clock off at 6 a.m. Back for midday."

"OK, I'm finishing off here and will join you shortly. See you soon," Abi dropped the call and walked over to Bill.

"Ok if I head off now, I need to write up my notes whilst they are still fresh."

"Sure, we'll be here for a few more hours. You waiting for the body to be collected?"

Abi hadn't intended to wait that long, but she took the invitation more as an instruction.

The coroner's van arrived around 45 minutes after the call. Two men, the driver and a passenger, got out of the van and looked up at the sky. The daylight had started, although the sunrise wasn't expected for another 30 minutes. They put on their white coveralls so as not to infect the evidence inside.

Abi looked over at them. Her father had died suddenly just over a year ago, he was young, still in his 50s. The doctor had visited, confirmed her death, and left the house with her father, now moved from the floor to the bed, lying peacefully. The doctor had explained that they could leave him there overnight and call the funeral director in the morning, but as time passed, her family was keen to have him moved to the funeral home. She had called the office number and was surprised that at two o clock in the morning, someone answered promptly. Less than an hour later, two men arrived at the house, neatly dressed in sombre suits. They offered their condolences, carefully wrapped her father in a body bag, and carried him to the car outside. The whole process was completed in less than 20 minutes.

She tried to prevent herself from smiling as she recalled the following morning, walking around the three funeral directors in her town as she was unsure which one she had called.

As she looked at the two men from the coroner's office, she thought of this moment and how people employed in the bereavement industry faced this situation daily. Even though it wasn't a close relative of anyone present, they still acknowledged the solemn occasion and treated the situation with dignity.

They walked over to Abi, assuming she was the attending detective, as they had recognised the others immediately.

"Do you want to take me through to the body?"

Abi donned a fresh pair of latex gloves and drew her coveralls up to her neck. She grabbed the camera, which was resting on the bonnet of her pool car. They walked indoors, where Sally was lying.

The two men unwrapped the body bag kit. This consisted of a body bag, a shroud kit, an instruction sheet, and labels. The body bag was unzipped and laid out flat on the carpet. Abi filmed the whole process, no one had told her what to film, so she assumed everything was the default. One carefully filled in the details on two of the labels, attaching one to her toe and the other through a strap on the body bag.

Between them, they lifted Sally, one gripping her shoulders and the other her feet, raising her slowly. Abi moved to the side as the body was raised to capture the armchair and the blood stains on the cushion where she was sitting. They moved Sally gently to the body bag and laid her flat, gripping the zip at the bottom and drawing it carefully along the length, Abi looked at her face disappearing as the zip was drawn.

One of them went back to the van and collected the stretcher, laying it parallel to the body. They then raised it onto the stretcher.

Finally, the stretcher was lifted and walked to the van, Eric opened the doors as he saw them approach, and the body was slid inside. The full procedure was completed in silence, with soundless signals between them throughout.

As the van drove off, Bill spoke to Abi.

"Are you heading off now?"

"Maybe, can you come and look at this with me?" Sally signalled Bill to join her.

They walked into the front room, the absence of Sally's body made it seem lighter, and the sunrise combined with the absence of the cadaver brightened the room.

Abi leaned over the armchair and pointed to the blood stain.

"Look closely. There is a large stain on the left-hand side of the chair."

Bill nodded, she knew where this was going.

"But also look at the small stain to the right of this," Bill said. The stain was only the size of a 10p piece. It wasn't the size, but the fact that it was separate from the main stain.

"The large stain was created by the blood from the head running down the left-hand side of the body, it could have spread across the surface of the cushion but hasn't, there must be a good six inches between the two stains. This stain would have been under her buttock."

As Abi spoke, Ben had placed a ruler on the cushion to provide scale and started to take pictures from all angles.

"Well spotted. Are you sure you want to go back to the station now, or do you want to hang around?" Bill said, detecting Abi's enthusiasm.

"I think I'll stay now, let me just buzz Chris," Abi walked away, picked up her phone, and called Chris.

"Hi, I think I'm going to hang around here for a couple more hours."

"You found something?" Chris's voice came across as a question. He was intrigued.

"Maybe. I'll let you know. See you later," Abi said, ending the call without waiting for a response.

Chris looked at his phone, she had hung up the call. Didn't even say goodbye. He knew this wasn't out of rudeness, they were close pals, and knew she had found something.

The notes that Chris had written up on the computer comprised a series of forms, most of which related to recording facts, such as timelines, addresses, and people present. It was a few forms in, and over one hour later, that he was able to describe in his own words what had happened. He knew that Abi would cover the situation from the house, but he recorded his observations just in case she missed anything.

The main thrust of his report was the short interview, it was less than 3 minutes long, and the reaction of James Gordon. He extended this to include the fact that his solicitor was there waiting when James was moved to the custody block and the reactions of the parties during the interview. The recording would capture the words, but there was just too much detail and unspoken body language that wasn't recorded.

As well as recording the facts, he was keen to record the unanswered questions while they were still fresh in his mind.

When did James call his solicitor? The phone records should confirm this.

The solicitor was smartly dressed and seemed very fresh, despite the time of day. This seemed strange.

Why did James take advice when read his rights, yet respond immediately when asked a direct question about the call?

What was said to end the interview so promptly?

Why didn't the solicitor want to spend time with his client before the interview?

He was just about to call it a day and log off the computer when another thought passed through his mind.

Why was James so calm?

He logged off the computer, stood up, and grabbed his jacket. It was 6.10 a.m.

"I thought I told you to be off for six Chris?"

The voice took him by surprise. The office had started to fill sometime before, but everyone got down to their work, and there was a gentle hum that got louder as more arrived. He turned and smiled, looking at his watch.

"Oh, come on. It's only ten past."

Detective Inspector Tom Christopher smiled back. "Only kidding, son, do you have a few minutes before you go? I promise you can be back for midday."

"Sure," he said, pulling a chair for his boss and sitting down.

"Ok, give me the quick rundown. It's the interview I'm interested in, Abi can fill me in with the rest."

The two sat together as Chris reeled off the details of the interview, explaining everything that was already in the notes.

"I think I'll pop over and interview him again. OK lad, off you go. See you back here at 12. No earlier, OK?"

Chris nodded, grabbed his jacket, and left.

Tom picked up the phone and called the custody suite.

"Hi there, Inspector Thomas. I'm calling about James Gordon. Is his solicitor still there?"

"No. He's just this second left, should I try and stop him?"

"No, that won't be necessary. Let him get home and rest, and call him in 30 minutes. I'll be there at 7 a.m."

Tom smiled at the thought of him getting home to find out he would be needed again right away.

Abi looked at the clock on the wall, it was showing just after 6 a.m. By her reckoning, she had been at the site for over 5 hours and had not left the living area. She would need a couple of hours to write up her notes and would like to overlap with Chris by at least an hour, so she figured on carrying on until 10 a.m. and then making her excuses.

Bill and Ben seemed oblivious to the time as they meticulously worked their way through the crime scene.

The house was an old-style cottage, the type that looked great from the side of the road or via the particulars on the estate agent's website. The reality was very different for anyone living there. Low ceilings, walls that failed to meet at right angles, period features that were impractical in the modern era, inadequate electricity sockets, and poor lighting that seemed to highlight dust in the few areas where the limited light met the surfaces.

Looking around the room Abi could see that most items had been in place for some time, except for items that are moved regularly, like the remote control for the TV and the bowl by the hallway that held the keys. As she looked into this bowl, she noticed two sets of car keys, one had a BMW fob, and the other was more generic, maybe a replacement set. As she came into the house, she noticed the BMW parked in the driveway, but other than the police vehicles, there was no other car. She started to ponder the absence of a second car, the house was remote, and it seemed reasonable that this would be a two-car family.

"Shall we take a quick walk around the rest of the house?" Bill called out.

A quick walk around the house seemed strange given the meticulous attention that had been applied to the living area where the body was found.

Seeing Abi's confusion, Bill explained. "The next team will be here in a couple of hours, they will do the detailed search. Let's see what we can find first.

Abi nodded and followed them into the kitchen area.

"This tends to elicit the least information for forensics," Ben started to explain, "People come and go all day and things are moved around all of the time. A knife in the kitchen doesn't look as ominous as one in the living room. Let's have a quick glance, I tend to look for things that are missing or in the wrong place."

As he spoke, Abi looked at the knife block. All of the knives were in place, none missing. As she looked at the matching plates lined up in the plate rack and the sink clear of washing, bar a single glass and a knife and fork, she thought of her bedsit and the evident 'crime scene'. What would forensics make of it?

Abi walked to the dishwasher and opened the door. It was mostly empty, except for the two plates, one wine glass, and one knife and

80

fork.

"Looks like the leftovers from an evening meal?"

Ben moved over and took pictures of the contents.

"Can you gently move the plates so I can take a picture," Ben spoke as he snapped away. "And let's bag these. No pans, so maybe this is from a takeaway?

Abi looked around for a bin and lifted the lid. There were two cardboard takeaway containers. She lifted the side and saw the brown sauce that covered the sides matched the contents of the plate.

"Bingo. Looks like they had a takeaway dinner, any labels on them?"

Abi lifted the box carefully so as not to tip the contents. Nothing on the lid or the sides.

"Nope. Should I bag these as well?" Asked the question of Ben.

"Yes please," Ben confirmed.

"We're missing a wine bottle," Abi said.

The bin was mostly empty, so a missing wine bottle was easy to see.

"Try the fridge, maybe they only drank half?"

"For red wine?" Abi questioned.

"OK, good point." Ben looked around the kitchen for a bottle. No sign. Try the recycling bin."

There was no sign of a recycling bin in the kitchen, a door off the kitchen led to a utility room. She walked in there and turned on the light. The room was used more as a junk space. Apart from a washing machine in one corner, the space was piled high with storage boxes, books, DVDs, and all the stuff that doesn't have a home. Good luck working through this lot.

Abi noticed a set of golf clubs.

"Does anyone know how many clubs are in a set?"

Two blank faces.

"Well, there are 17 here, does that seem correct?"

Bill and Ben shrugged.

Chapter Five

The barriers rose as Tom arrived at the custody suite, the receptionist recognised the car. As he approached the door, the buzzer clicked and let him in. No need for the security check, he had been coming here for over a decade, and woe betide anyone who hadn't recognised him.

"Hi Tom, I thought you were planning to call ahead to get the solicitor?" The duty receptionist seemed concerned that Tom had arrived and would now be waiting.

"I decided that I could do with some time to read the reports first, do you want to ask Mr. Gordon if he wants a solicitor present? I think we can guess the answer."

The receptionist nodded and went to the cell, he returned less than a minute later.

"Yup, you're right. I'll call him now."

"I don't suppose the quality of the drinks has improved here, have they?"

It was a rhetorical question, one that Tom had asked every time he came. He grabbed the brown liquid in a small plastic cup and headed to the office to read his notes. Twenty minutes later, there was a tap on the door.

"He's here."

"Ok, on my way."

Tom walked into the main area and stared at the besuited gentleman, immaculately dressed. He didn't recognise him, which he found strange after so many years on the job, he thought he knew all of the Brighton solicitors. The gentleman stood up and walked towards Tom, holding his palm flat to the ground. Tom grabbed it and moved 90 degrees to try and turn his wrist. Two alpha males were trying to assert their authority.

"Detective Inspector Tom Christopher. I don't think I've had the pleasure?"

"Charles Beadle, no, I don't think we have met before," Charles refused to give anything away and relished in the fact that he was a new face to Tom.

"Before we start, can you please confirm that you don't wish to speak to your client alone?" The implication was that Tom did not want to play the same games that wrong-footed Chris earlier.

"No, Inspector. Let's get straight to it shall we?"

The two men walked to the questioning room, where James was already seated. Without ceremony, Tom unwrapped and inserted the cassettes, looked at the clock and pressed play.

"The time is 7.15 a.m. on Sunday 14th July. Present are James Gordon, his solicitor, Charles Beadle and myself, Detective Inspector Tom Christopher"

"Tom Christopher," James laughed. "Earlier, I had Detective Chris Thomas. Who makes these things up?"

Tom ignored James and quickly read his rights.

"Are you clear?"

No response

"Mr. Gordon, I will ask you again, are you clear?" Tom had over twenty years of experience in interviews, he held his calm and tried to assert his authority.

"Ready to roll, Inspector."

"Thank you. First of all, I would like to establish what you were doing yesterday up to the point that you called 999," Tom wasn't going to be drawn into the wording of the call just yet.

"You want me to start with yesterday?"

Tom nodded.

"Well, I woke up around 8 a.m. Sally brought me breakfast in bed, as it was my birthday," James paused, "I guess you're not going to wish me a happy birthday for yesterday then?"

Tom remained passive. James held the silence for a bit longer."

"I guess not then. Oh well, it wasn't the best of birthdays, was it? I got up around 8.30, the three S's and then headed downstairs. I guess around 9 a.m. I read the paper and then did the crossword for a couple of hours."

Tom held firm, Gordon knew when he asked for his whereabouts the day before that he wanted to know about the time around Sally's murder and that news of a shit, shower and shave was just stalling.

"I then drove into Brighton and met a couple of friends."

Tom interrupted, "Can you provide the names and numbers of these friends please?"

"Of course," Tom was expecting him to write down the names and was surprised when his solicitor passed a piece of paper with the names and phone numbers pre-prepared.

"We had a quick drink and a chat in Brighton at the Black Lion. Don't worry, Inspector, I only had a couple so I wasn't over the limit."

"Can you confirm where you parked, sir?"

"I can describe where I parked, I have used the same spot for years, but I have no idea what it is called. I paid in cash, so won't have a record."

"Can you confirm your registration number so we can confirm?" The myriad of cameras around Brighton would confirm his statement.

James provided the registration number.

"I guess that I was in the pub until around 2 p.m., I didn't think to check. I went and did a bit of shopping, just bits and bobs, and then left around 3 p.m. and drove home."

Tom made a few notes, most would be on the recording, so these were more questions for later. He was hopeful that the parking ticket would confirm the time of arrival and departure as registration numbers were captured at entry and exit.

"I drove home over via Ditchling Beacon, stopping for a short walk, and then arrived home around 4 p.m. Do you need all of this detail, Inspector?"

Tom nodded again, James realised this was the extent of his acknowledgment. Charles sat beside him, totally impassive. He must have gone through the story several times, the fact that Charles never even blinked suggested that he was sticking to a script.

"I got home around 4 p.m., Sally was waiting. She made me a cup of tea. We had a chat. At 7 p.m. Sally went out to collect a takeaway."

"Which takeaway?" It was the first real question to Gordon's monologue, and Tom had cut him off mid-sentence.

"Erm, I'm unsure, Inspector. We don't get deliveries around our way, so we have to drive and collect. I had a glass of wine on top of my two beers, so Sally drove and I stayed at home."

Charles blinked. Tom noticed, and Charles noticed that he had noticed.

"And what time did she return?" Just like before, Tom jumped in with the question straight away.

"Difficult to say, maybe 45 minutes later."

"And what were you doing during this time?"

"I was watching TV, Inspector."

"What were you watching?" James was rapidly approaching the likely period of Sally's death, and Tom's questions came fast.

"Buggered if I know, just flicking through Netflix looking for something to watch."

James was noticeably relaxed, he was back to the script now. Again, Tom noticed the change in demeanour and made a note.

"So she returned at 7.45 p.m. You ate straight away?"

"Yes. She had laid out the plates. She served the takeaway, something spicy in case you want to know. We sat down and ate and shared a bottle of red wine."

"And what did you talk about?"

Charles blinked again, another diversion from the script Tom suspected.

"Oh, I don't know. We have been married for 16 years Inspector. Do couples still chat after so long?"

James looked at Tom expecting a response. None was forthcoming.

"Maybe we talked about the kids, school fees, and all the usual stuff that couples discuss, I'm not sure."

Tom sat impassively.

"And then we finished."

"What time?"

"I guess around 8.30 p.m., and then went upstairs to the bedroom. It's my birthday Inspector," James winked as he said the words.

"We had a bit of rumpy-pumpy, she let me do her up the wrong 'un. As I said, it was my birthday."

"So after sex, did you stay in bed?"

"Yes, Inspector, we laid in each other's arms, whispering sweet nothings."

"After 16 years of marriage, it's good to hear the spark is still there."

Charles blinked again.

"Yes, Inspector, the spark was still there." James answered the question honestly, his eyes noticeably welled.

Tom noticed the sadness in his eyes, the first time he saw the real James Gordon. He pressed on with the questioning.

"And then what?"

"And then, inspector, we got up, got dressed, and went downstairs. I guess this was around 9.30."

James looked Tom directly in the eye as he spoke.

"And then I killed her."

Tom blinked.

❖

The sunrise was sometime before, the sun that had shone through the kitchen window had now moved high in the sky. The freshness of the morning was slowly giving way to the heat of the sun, Abi looked at her watch, 9.45 a.m., and was beginning to question the wisdom of her decision to remain with the forensic team as she stifled a yawn.

They had moved upstairs after capturing most of the downstairs.

"More of a photography and video exercise," Bill suggested that there would be few clues to be found upstairs.

The top floor consisted of four bedrooms and a bathroom. The doors were open, and before the question was asked, Abi answered any possible confusion, "Chris told me he opened the doors earlier looking for any other people in the house."

Bill and Ben acknowledged with a grunt.

They quickly scanned the landing and recognised the master bedroom as the largest room not encumbered by toys and computer games. Bill was filming while Ben was clicking away on the camera.

On the floor lay a couple of large cushions, far too big to be used as pillows and most likely decorative.

"I suspect the cushions were on the bed and were removed so the quilt cover could be taken off," Bill muttered to no one in particular, but was keen for her initial observations to be recorded.

"The quilt cover over Sally?" Abi asked the question to no one in particular, again just to record the observation.

"That's my guess," Bill chose to answer the question regardless.

"It's a very clean room, if this were mine there would be clothes lying everywhere. Apart from the two cushions, this could be part of a show home," Ben declared.

Ben lifted the cover that draped over the sides of the bed to allow Bill to film underneath before taking pictures himself. He stood on his tiptoes, and pointed the camera to the top of the wardrobe, and clicked twice before reviewing the pictures on the small screen.

"Nothing, not even dust."

They looked at the ensuite bathroom, which was again freshly cleaned. The towels were neatly folded over the racks, and even the toilet roll had been folded into a neat point.

"I don't think we are going to glean anything from this room. Let's take a quick look at the others," Ben said as he backed out of the bedroom onto the landing. They quickly checked the kid's rooms, neither of which were messy, and tidied after the kids had left. The main bathroom looked unused and as fresh as the ensuite.

As they backed out onto the hallway, Ben looked at the ceiling and noticed a loft door. He stood, focusing on the door, before pointing to Abi.

"Look closely at the edge there," he paused as Abi stared at the seemingly bland door, "see the painting, whenever this was painted, and it has started to yellow already, they painted too close to the edge. If the door was opened the paint would crack. I think we can skip that for now, but I suggest you check the contents with the next team."

Abi nodded and then looked at the remaining room.

"This must be James' office. Refreshing to see some sign of activity," Bill said as she walked in filming, the room looked organised but used. Most paper was stacked in neat piles or trays, a couple of sheets sat at an angle.

"What's in the filing cabinets?" Abi mused as she opened the top drawer of the filing cabinet and saw carefully labelled sections marked Electricity, Gas, Water, etc. Ben and Bill were filming and capturing the scene as the drawer was opened and the contents viewed. She opened the second drawer.

"Empty," she turned to the bottom drawer, "also empty." Abi stood up and looked at the desk.

"How tall was Sally?" Abi asked the question, it seemed out of place.

"I dunno, 5 foot something, I guess. She's not that tall," Ben chimed in with an answer.

"The lower 5 foot, I think. She had small feet. Why do you ask?" Bill offered her opinion.

"The seat is set pretty low. I would guess that this is Sally's office. She was pretty short, as I recall, if the seat was any higher, her feet wouldn't touch the ground. I guess we don't know how tall her husband is?"

Two shakes of the head.

"And the extra chair?" Bill pointed to the dining room chair. "Maybe James and her were working on something together?"

The question lingered.

"OK, let's work on the assumption that this is Sally's office. And …. we seem to be missing a computer," their attention was drawn to the monitor on the desk. It was a large screen sporting an Apple logo.

"It's just a monitor. I suspect that she attached this to a laptop," Abi continued her observation.

Bill bent down and looked under the desk. "Looks like there is a loose cable." She leaned under the desk and pushed the cable up the back, Abi grabbed the end and studied it.

"Yes, that's the monitor cable."

"Fuck!" The desk shook as Bill attempted to back out of the underside of the desk.

"What's happened?"

"Nothing. Just banged my bloody head. Oh, wait, what do we have here? Can you take a couple of shots?"

Ben leaned down, pointing the camera at the underside of the desk. A piece of paper, let's see what it says," Ben signalled that he had the shot and Bill tugged at the sheet. She backed out again, this time careful not to knock her head.

"Brunswick Haulage, Balcombe, East Sussex. It looks like an invoice. Delivery of goods to Skipsea, £22,000. Wow, that must have been some delivery. It's dated two years ago."

Tom regained his composure and looked at James. He had heard many a confession over his years as a detective, with murderers looking him in the eye as they coldly described their deeds in detail. Some get a kick from this moment, possibly the last time they will be in the spotlight describing their show. Most would choose silence or play down their crime when in court to help reduce the sentence.

Let them have their moment, Tom thought.

"And how did you kill Sally, Mr. Gordon?"

"With the hockey stick, of course."

The mention of the hockey stick was news to Tom, a detail, if known to Chris, that was missed in their rushed handover a couple of hours before. He remained impassive, not willing to give away his lack of knowledge of the weapon to James.

"Of course. And how did you use the stick?"

James gestured with his arms as he demonstrated a swinging action.

"Sally was sat in the armchair, I threw the quilt cover over her head, and I swung the stick like this. This stick hit her just below the ear, and she went silent. I checked her pulse, and two minutes later she was dead."

James spoke the words eloquently, emphasising the vowels, as he had throughout the interview, in the same voice as he had earlier spoken his name and described having sex with Sally.

"Just the once?"

"Yes, Detective Inspector, just the once."

"And why did you do this, Mr. Gordon?"

"To kill her detective inspector, to kill her. I wanted her dead."

"That was a good shot."

"I'm sorry, detective inspector. What was a good shot? This hardly seems an appropriate thing to say as my client is describing the killing of his wife," Charles chipped in instinctively, breaking his silence.

Tom ignored Charles's comments and repeated the words, looking James in the eye as he emphasised the vowels, mimicking his clipped tone.

"I said, that was a good shot."

James looked at Charles for advice, none was forthcoming, and returned his gaze to Tom.

"I'm not sure what you mean. A good shot?"

"Yes, a good shot. Sally had a quilt cover over her head and you managed to swing a ….," he looked at his notes, "a hockey stick at her and struck her right across the ear. This is the weakest part of the skull. Anywhere else and you would have just bruised her. But you found the spot in a single blow."

James looked at Charles again for advice, but Charles ignored his glare. James closed his eyes for a couple of seconds, as if to consider his response, looked Tom in the eye, and spoke.

"Yes, I guess I got lucky, Detective Inspector," James chose not to correct his assumption that the quilt cover was over her at the time of the blow.

Chris was buzzing. He had returned to his apartment just after 7.30 a.m., thankfully he lived local to the station. He had showered, set his alarm for 11.30 a.m. and layed down for a nap, passing out almost immediately.

Thirty minutes later, he was wide awake.

He had dreamed about the case and sat bolt upright as the details went through his mind. He tossed and turned for another 30 minutes before giving in. He knew sleep was unlikely, so settled on rest instead. He searched on his phone for some meditation videos and was drawn to the website called Soul Writing, where he found a meditation that took him through a labyrinth. He played a couple more meditation exercises from the same site and then dragged himself out of bed around 10 a.m. His body felt relaxed but he was still tired, so he put on some coffee and added a couple of extra spoonfuls to the filter.

Two litres of expresso-strength coffee and a shower later, he was walking back to the station that he had only left four and a half hours earlier, deliberately walking slowly so as not to arrive before midday.

"You made it before me, I see?" He had spotted Abi's back to him as he walked into the office, she must be as keen as he was.

"This lady is under strict instructions to head home soon," Tom stood behind Chris and walked over to Abi carrying two cups of coffee."

"She is still on Saturday time, and, if she doesn't leave soon, HR will have my bollocks for earrings," Tom spoke the words with a smile in his voice but his face showed he was serious.

"Let's have a quick debrief, and then I will be calling you a taxi."

Abi started to protest but realised this wasn't open to negotiation.

"Grab yourself a coffee, Chris, and I'll see you in room 4."

Abi talked them through the forensic search, and Tom was making notes in his notepad and adding bullet points to the whiteboard at the same time. She finished and was amazed at how many pages of notes had been produced.

"And your interview?" She looked at Tom, her eyes begging to be able to stay.

"And my interview will be available and written up by 8 a.m. when you next come to the station tomorrow," the firmness in Tom's voice made it clear that this was not up for negotiation.

"Alright, I'll see you then. Call me if you need me."

"And turn your bloody phone off Abi. You're no use to me tired. Chris here looks as though it's only the caffeine that is keeping him awake," Tom stared at a sheepish-looking Chris, "You're going to have a blinder of a headache by the end of the day."

Abi nodded, strode to her desk to collect her belongings, and headed out of the door, Chris and Tom watched her until she walked out the main entrance.

"OK, this should be a straightforward case. We have a dead body, and a confession, and, as far as I can see, the evidence to back it up. I would like to drive him to Lewes this afternoon and lock him away, but there are procedures to follow and a case to prepare, so let's get this right," Tom knew that they had a few weeks of work ahead of them, the sooner this was started, the better.

"Sure, boss, what do you want me to do?"

"Well, there's no shortage of things to do today, I suggest you start by popping along to Offham and taking a fresh look at the house, the second team should be there by now. The coroner should be able to provide an initial report on the body today, I'll call you when this is ready, and we can go and visit together. We also need to knock on some doors for statements."

"Well, that should be easy. We'll be pushed to find more than a dozen doors within half a mile."

"I was going to say we will get someone from uniform to help, but it looks as though you will be able to handle this yourself," Tom smiled as he spoke, he could see Chris already regretting his comment.

❖

The last time Chris had driven to the house, it was just past midnight, and, apart from the moonlight and a few stars in the sky, it was dark. Now, as he drove back to the house over Ditchling Beacon the sun was high in the sky and lit up the beautiful Sussex countryside. After serving his first few years in London he felt so happy breathing in the relatively clearer air and taking in the tapestry of colours that the Downs had to offer. As he slowed down to turn left to Offham he looked at the Blacksmith Arms on his right and recognised the telltale panel indicating that Harvey's beer was sold there. He wasn't a fan, but Abi was. She routinely pointed out the pubs that sold the beer, and he wondered if she knew about this one.

A few minutes later he drew up outside the house, the police officer detailed to keep an eye on the premises had changed, and he recognised him straight away as they had trained together as probationers.

"Hello Phil, did you draw the short straw again?"

"Well, if it ain't Morse. I suppose you have solved this one already?"

The banter was friendly, Chris got out of the car and hugged his friend.

"Not while we're on duty, darling, people will talk," Phil laughed as he pushed him away. "I have just received a call that the forensic team is delayed and expected here for 3 p.m."

Chris looked at his watch, the time was 1.50 p.m, over an hour to wait.

"Guess I will be door-knocking then."

The two shared a few more words before he walked back to his car and got out his phone and loaded Maps. Within a couple of seconds the app had located him by the house. He zoomed out to see what houses were nearby, made notes, and started the car for the first on his list.

Maybe it was the time of day, but most houses that he knocked at elicited no reply. Two were answered by the cleaner, who was questioned. Only in three houses was the owner present. Out of the 18 houses on his list, he had spoken to five people and had to plan to revisit the rest later on.

The questions were routine, did they know James and Sally Gordon? Did they see or hear anything suspicious? Could they contact him if they recalled any further details? As the case was still to make the local news, the residents questioned had more questions of their own, all of which were deflected with the expertise of a politician.

His phone pinged, he looked at the screen and saw a message from Phil.

"Forensics just arrived, you on your way?"

Chris quickly composed a reply, "On my way. Should be 5 minutes." He started the car and set off, less than four minutes later, he was back outside of the house.

One of the forensics officers was waiting by the door; Chris didn't recognise him, they called over to him.

"Get yourself suited and booted son."

Chris got out of his car and went to the boot to get out the equipment. He looked down and noticed the plastic bag by the hedge. He moved closer to take a look, bending down.

"Have you found something?" The forensic officer looked over at him.

"Not sure, best take a few pictures and bag this," he took out his mobile phone and snapped away from different angles. He then grabbed an evidence bag, and carefully lifted the item and sealed it. He marked the label and passed it to his colleague.

"Probably nothing."

Chris returned to his car to suit and boot up, and just as he finished, his phone rang. He answered.

"You busy?" It was Tom.

Chris considered his situation, if he were inside, he might have said yes, but as he was still to join the forensic team he decided he was free.

"I guess not."

"Good, see you at the mortuary. Apparently, there are a few questions on this one."

In the late 1970s, a small, sleazy cinema, called the Vogue, used to play sex films and host striptease evenings. When this went bust, it was taken over as a family venture, playing classic and children's films. The venture lasted only a few months before also going bust. It remained closed and was demolished in the early 80s for a road widening scheme, known to the Brighton locals as the Vogue Gyratory. A sad ending for a grand building that started back in the 1930s with all the glitz and glamour of a Fred Astaire and Ginger Rogers film.

To reach the Brighton mortuary, one has to navigate this gyratory system and then move rapidly to the left-hand lane to enter the Woodvale cemetery. As Chris tried to move over, an impatient white van driver drove up the inside blasting his horn. Chris was tempted to record his registration number, but that would be spiteful, so ignored it.

As he drove towards the mortuary, respecting the 15 mph speed limit, he recognised Tom's car and pulled up alongside. He walked towards the entrance and saw Tom sitting outside, waiting.

"They're not quite ready for us yet. Let's enjoy the sunshine for a few minutes. How did you get on?"

Chris assumed he meant the door knocking.

"Well, I visited 18 houses and spoke to two cleaners and three residents. No one heard anything, and not a single one of them knew James or Sally. I will have to pop back later when they're home, I guess?" His eyes pleaded with Tom for someone else to be assigned this fruitless task.

"I didn't expect anything else, to be honest. Yes, pop back there and try again after we see the guys."

Tom had done his door knocking over the years, a necessary evil that Chris would just have to get used to.

"Anything else?"

Chris thought. "Not really, I was ready to join forensics when you called, so I didn't get inside. Oh, I found a plastic bag," he jokingly said, bigging up the plastic bag.

"Well done you. You'll be surprised just how many crimes hinge on small details like this. Don't diss it just yet."

The door behind them opened.

"Tom, we're ready for you," he said, looking at Chris, "Sorry, I don't think we have met?"

"Chris Thomas, nice to meet you," he held out his hand.

"Chris Thomas and Tom Christopher," he laughed. "You can't make this up"

He looked at Tom who grimaced

"Believe me, once I find the prat in HR that fixed me up with this, I will send them down for five years!" Tom was starting to get bored with the joke, but clearly he was alone.

As they donned the gowns and face masks, Chris started to question just how many times a day he had to go through this process. Twice at the crime scene and again at the mortuary. He will no doubt return to Offham later and repeat the exercise. At least the face masks seemed routine, the COVID situation a year ago made these things commonplace.

As they walked into the chilled room they saw Sally's body lying on the stainless steel surface, a block of wood under her neck, and a small piece of cloth covering her pubic area, offering some dignity. An inverted Y-shaped scar ran down her torso, which had been roughly stitched up. Skin can't heal after death, so pointless trying to apply tidier stitches.

The pathologist started immediately, with no time for pleasantries.

"The deceased, Sally Gordon. She died from serious trauma caused by a single blow to her left temple. The skull is weakest here and shattered with the impact of the blow. She didn't die immediately, I would guess on around three hours, maybe four before she died. The estimated time of death is 8 p.m."

"8 p.m?" Chris wasn't au fait with the protocol in these sessions. Maybe it was a mistake to interrupt, but he wanted to to ask all the same.

"Yes, 8 p.m. If I may continue?"

Tom gave Chris the dagger's look. The pathologist continued.

"Estimated time of death, 8 p.m. As I say, she was left to die for around three hours. She would have been unconscious during this period, the blow was fatal, and a surgeon would have struggled to fix this. At least not leaving her a quality of life. I would say this was a well-placed hit by someone with experience or a lucky shot."

"That was a good shot," Tom recalled his conversation with James earlier. His comment wasn't a question and was ignored.

"There are no other obvious injuries. We can tell she ate a salad around four hours before her death, and traces of semen between her buttocks suggest she had sex in the hours before her death. We have sent samples to the labs for testing, but expect them to match James Gordon's DNA."

"She let me do her up the wrong 'un," Tom again muttered a comment from his interview with James.

"I'm sorry Inspector?" The pathologist was able to ignore Tom's initial comment, but couldn't ignore this one.

"She let me do her up the wrong 'un. When I interviewed James Gordon, he said these words. Seemed strange at the time to mention such a detail. Do you have any evidence that Sally Gordon had anal sex before she was killed?"

"That would be difficult to prove unless it was immediately before the death. The presence of semen doesn't prove this one way or another."

"Surely she would have washed, either way?" Chris realised that it had moved from a monologue to an open discussion, and he had questions of his own.

"I can't imagine it would be comfortable to go unwashed, that's for sure. But if you ask me as a pathologist, I can only state what I can see. Shall we move on?"

The monologue continued, including details of the body temperature and the background to the estimate of time of death. Details of food in her intestines, detailed explanations of the wound, and how the estimates of how long she had taken to die had been calculated. Tom and Chris took notes as he spoke.

The body was moved to show the injuries and other observations. As the body was turned over Chris made another comment and underlined it.

Santorum.

They moved out of the chilled area and removed their gowns and face masks. They exchanged pleasantries and started to move to the door to exit. Tom stopped.

"Quick question, sorry if you don't have it to hand, but you mentioned the contents of the stomach. You didn't mention any wine or alcohol."

"Sorry, I forgot to mention what wasn't present. I should have confirmed that there was no alcohol in her digestive tract."

"And the presence of alcohol is easy to confirm, I assume?" Tom knew the answer but asked for confirmation and to make sure that Chris understood.

"Yes, very easy, Inspector. There was no alcohol in her digestive tract or her blood."

"Sorry son, I hadn't meant to stop you when I did. It's just that some of the pathologists, and this one in particular, are very precise in their processes. Lecture first, and then questions after. You saw how he even stopped me?"

"No problem, but thanks, there's a first time for everything. Another lesson learned and another personality flagged."

A lot of those in the station saw Tom as having an offish personality, but Chris and Abi didn't feel this at all. His semi-apology added more substance to their opinion. Both of them saw in Tom a detective with years of experience and close to retirement, trying to hand over the baton to the next generation.

"Any thoughts? Spit them out while they are fresh in your mind," Tom suspected that Chris was holding back a question, he had noticed him forcefully underline a word while he wrote the notes and was surprised he hadn't followed up with a question.

"Santorum."

"What?"

"Santorum. A few years ago, a US Senator named Rich Santorum upset a lot of people with his views on homosexuality and same-sex marriage. He pissed off a lot of people at the time."

Tom looked confused, "I want to say get to the fucking point, but I think you want to give me some history on the US Senate. So go on, but do get to the point soon. Please!"

Chris only heard the bit about him lecturing the US Senate, so he chose to continue in this vein.

"So Rich Santorum pissed off a lot of people and a lot of voters. Needless to say, he is now an ex-Senator. But that isn't my point."

Tom looked relieved.

"For a word to receive a dictionary definition, it needs to appear in several publications, like books, newspapers, and magazines, and also be used widely in the same way across the internet."

Tom started to look less relieved.

"So this journalist called Dan Savage started a campaign. Create a definition for the word 'Santorum' and then use it so often that it becomes a recognised definition."

"And I assume this Savage guy was successful?" Tom was still unsure where this was going.

"Google it and see. It will be the first hit."

Tom picked up his phone, loaded the browser, and started to type the word. He looked up Chris for help.

"S-A-N-T-O-R-U-M," Chris guessed the question.

It wasn't the first hit, supporters of Rich Santorum had acted as diligently as Savage in trying to change the search order, but it was one of the top hits. Tom saw the entry, 'What does Santorum mean?' He started to read.

"Oh, you sick fucker. Why did you send me here?" He looked up at Chris expecting a smile; he had been led to many a dodgy link by colleagues in the past and assumed this was a joke. But Chris wasn't smiling.

"Sally was clean. She didn't have anal sex."

"And she hadn't drunk alcohol or had anything spicy either. What is he playing at?"

Tom and Chris spoke for a bit longer before splitting up.

Tom drove to the station, and Chris headed back to Offham to complete the door-knocking. Chris had started to wilt; he had been awake for nearly 36 hours, save a couple of hours meditating.

"Complete the door knocking, come back to the station, and write up the notes. Then get to bed. I will see you at 8 a.m. tomorrow."

Arriving back in Offham Chris looked at his notes and worked out a rough order for the remaining 15 houses. Another fruitless exercise, six of the residents were at home but had never met or seen Sally. He crossed off the houses he had visited and created a new list of those he still had to visit, a task for tomorrow. He got back in his car and started the drive to the station.

As he reached the top of the ramp by Offham Church, he indicated left to turn into Lewes and looked right to see if the road was clear. He saw the pub, flipped his indicators, turned right, and then parked behind the pub.

It was early evening, and the pub was still busy with customers eating Sunday dinners. A couple with two small dogs (were they Italian Greyhounds?) queued at the bar. Chris stood behind them, waiting. The man reached into the jar with doggie biscuits, grabbed a few, and placed them in his pocket. The barman gave them their drinks, and they moved to seats in the corner. The dogs had smelled the biscuits and were jumping up at the man in expectation.

"Sorry to trouble you, I can see you're very busy. Any chance we could talk?" Chris spoke softly, he didn't want to alert everyone in the pub as he showed the barman his warrant card.

The barman lifted his wrists towards Chris, his smile stretching from ear to ear. Chris felt, embarrassed and the barman's smile spread wider.

"I'm only dissing you. Fitz," he said, holding out his hand to Chris.

"Chris," first names seemed to be in order.

"Grab a seat over there," Fitz pointed, "I will be with you in two minutes. Can I get you a drink?"

Chris nodded, "Thanks, but."

"But, you're on duty," Fitz grinned again.

"Yes, I'm on duty," Chris moved to the chair and waited.

Fitz returned to the kitchen, grabbed some plates, and walked them over to some customers. He exchanged pleasantries with them before returning to the bar. Two minutes later, he was sitting in front of Chris.

"How may I help you, Chris?"

Chris took out his phone and searched for the picture he had taken the night before.

"Do you recognise any of the people in the picture?" He offered the phone to Fitz who zoomed in.

"I don't recognise the man, but the woman comes in here most weeks with a group of friends. I think they are a retired sports group, hockey or something like that."

His eyes lit up on the word 'hockey' and he thought back to the hockey stick they had found under the settee.

"You say a retired sports group?"

"Yes, the same group of women have been coming here for a couple of years. Initially, they were all in their sports gear, but gradually more and more of them turned up in their normal gear. I guess that they dropped out one by one, but still came for the drinks and chat."

"And Sally, the lady in the picture, has been coming for years as well?"

"Mostly. She joined them a few years ago, initially irregularly. For the past two years, she has been one of the regulars, I would say."

Chris was making notes, the group of women would be helpful to trace, and they would be able to say more about Sally.

"And her husband?"

Fitz looked closer at the picture. He didn't recognise James at all. "Nope, I've not seen him here."

"I don't suppose you have any names or contact details, do you?" Chris realised this was a fruitless exercise, most people go by first names in pubs, as his experience demonstrated, but it was worth asking all the same.

"Well, that's one thing we can be thankful to COVID for. People used to call in to book tables and never turned up. It seemed wrong to demand, or even record, a phone number each time, but COVID made this a requirement."

Fitz stood up and went to the bar to collect the booking diary. He returned, flipping through the pages.

"There we go, the name is Carol. She always books Tuesdays," he read out her number.

"Thanks, that's most helpful."

"No problem at all, I can ask around if anyone else knows anything.

Do you think I can have a copy of the picture?"

Chris hesitated, "Probably not, sorry. I snapped this in the house. It isn't an official photo, and, well."

Fitz stopped him, 'No problem. I'll start with the bar staff and see if they know her."

Chris offered him his card, "Ok if I pop back later? In the meantime, if you hear anything?"

"Of course, see you soon."

The phone rang twice before Carol answered.

"Hello, Carol speaking."

"Hello, Carol. My name is Detective Thomson. Sorry to call out of the blue. I understand you are a friend of Sally Gordon."

"Yes, why? Has something happened to Sally?" Carol's voice started to tremble as she spoke Sally's name.

Chris didn't answer directly. 'Would it be possible to come over and chat?"

"Of course," Carol gave her address.

The address was in Lewes, Chris estimated a 15-minute drive. He looked at his watch.

"Thank you. I will see you around 18.30 if that's OK?"

"Yes, of course. Is Sally OK?"

"I can explain shortly. I will see you in 15 minutes."

Chris entered the address into the maps application, and it directed him to an address east of Lewes in the Malling area. Ten minutes later, he was outside the house. Carol, who must have been watching through the window, opened the door as soon as the stranger's car parked. He locked the door and walked towards her.

"Is Sally alright?" Carol looked shocked, Chris tried to delay an answer until they got indoors.

"I'm sorry to say that Sally Gordon was killed, I mean murdered, yesterday. We have a suspect in custody."

"Oh my God," she said, throwing her head into her hands and starting to crying.

"And James? Is he OK? He must be distraught?"

The word 'distraught' was a new one on Chris. The James he had met was cold and calculated, in the short period that he had met James, he didn't detect any feelings between James and Sally. 'I have just killed my wife, Sally'. Chris still recalled the tone of the first time he spoke to James, he certainly detected no warmth.

"I'm not sure, Carol. Were James and Sally close?"

"They were like two young lovers over the past couple of years. James' business was on the up, and they moved into their dream home. The kids went to private school, and the two of them made the most of their time together. Can I talk to him, please?"

"I'm not sure if that is possible," James was still to be charged, and it would be wrong to identify him as the prime suspect at this stage.

"We have specialist people keeping an eye on James, so I wouldn't worry,"

Chris wasn't lying, the 'specialist people' were a team of custody staff, but they were keeping a close eye on him.

Chris continued, "You say James' business was on the up recently? What is the name of the business?"

"Brunswick Haulage."

The name was not unknown to Chris. The Brunswick pub in Hove was one of his regular haunts, but he doubted the two were related.

He continued to quiz Carol for another 30 minutes, making notes. She spoke of the relationship between Sally and James, it sounded idyllic, and given the closeness of Sally and Carol there was no reason for her to lie about this.

Chris was just about to leave when he asked a final question.

"Fitz, the landlord at the Blacksmiths, says that there is a large group of you that go for the hockey evening. Do you have their names and contact details?"

"Lacrosse, not hockey. A lot of people get these confused, most don't even know what lacrosse is. Let me get you their numbers," Carol picked up her phone and went through the directory, calling out the details.

Just as Chris was leaving Carol's, the 'shit hit the fan'.

Tom was expecting a call from the crime reporter at the Argus and had a series of comments prepared that provided the minimum information required by law. Although James was in custody and had confessed to killing Sally, he was still to be charged and therefore was offered a small level of anonymity. The law allowed suspects to be held for 36 to 96 hours on serious charges like murder, so the onus was on the police to get as many facts together as possible, before officially charging.

"Detective Inspector Christopher. I understand that you have James Gordon in custody for the murder of his wife, Sally. Would you like to comment?" The Argus reporter hit Tom with the details right away.

"At this stage, we have a suspect in custody. Investigations are underway, and we will release further details once they are available," in over twenty years of service, Tom had handled many a call like this. He always refused the familiarity that most of the journalists offered and strictly toed the official line.

"So I understand, Inspector. I also understand that Sally was hit across her left temple by a hockey stick. Would you like to comment?"

Tom nearly spat out the coffee he was sipping. The mention of the hockey stick was still speculation to the police and no one outside of the immediate team was aware of such a detail. Someone must have leaked the story to the newspaper. He quickly discounted any of the immediate team; this simply wasn't possible.

"As I say. Investigations are underway, and we will release further details once they are available."

"Inspector, we will be running the story in a couple of hours. Would you care to add anything more?"

Tom was more than happy to add a lot more, but his professionalism prevented him from repeating the words in his mind.

"If that is so, would you do me the decency of sending me the article?"

"It's in your mailbox now," As the journalist spoke, Tom's mail pinged as a new email was received.

"Thank you. We will be issuing a statement shortly, goodbye," Tom ended the call. He looked up just as Chris entered the office.

Tom's face was in a rage. He opened the email and browsed the screen. Pictures of James and Sally on their wedding day, pictures of them happy on holiday. Two smiling people, the headline;

"Police suspect James Gordon of killing his wife Sally."

Chris knew better than to talk, and Tom's rages were short-lived. Let him ride this one out and then talk. He looked over Tom's shoulder and read the article with him.

"Killed with a blow by a hockey stick. How the fuck do they know this? We have yet to even prove this?"

"Lacrosse. Sally didn't play hockey, she played lacrosse," Chris's thoughts went back to his earlier conversation with Carol.

"Lacrosse? What is lacrosse?"

"It's a game, a bit like hockey. The stick has a net where the players can pick up the ball and hurl it across the pitch. I know you're going to ask me why I'm telling you this?" Chris knew Tom's personality too well, "I had to wiki it myself. The question is, why did we find a hockey stick? Maybe Sally played both? But her friend didn't suggest this was the case. And I don't think it was James', I don't think he plays hockey. Just a guess, of course, and I will follow up."

Tom smiled and said, "Good work, son. We'll make a detective out of you yet."

He looked at his watch, it was 19.30. "Get your notes written up. Let's meet again at 6 a.m., can you text Abi to be in early? I'm off to chat with Mr. Gordon."

Chapter Six

Abi kept her phone on silent, but left it on charge by her bed. She woke up and headed to the bathroom, stumbling back into bed. She tried to resist the temptation to look at her phone but was curious to see if there was a response from her recent date, to whom she had sent a quick, and rather suggestive, message before going to sleep.

He was still listed as 'Bumble' in her address book, and she had only met him twice. Abi was told that police work didn't go well alongside having a life, and she was rapidly realising this was the case. They had planned to meet for a drink on Sunday evening, but she was too tired. A simple message to say sorry might be the last message she could send him, so decided to up the ante and keep him interested, She unlocked the screen and scrolled through her messages. She smiled as she read Bumble's response.

'Breakfast sounds perfect. I'll bring my toothbrush xx'

She made a note to reply to him. Breakfast it will have to be now that she was on a murder investigation. She flicked through her other messages and saw the message from Chris.

"The boss wants us in for 6 a.m. Fancy breakfast at the Market Diner? See you at 5.15 a.m."

She looked at the time on her phone, it was 4.30. It looked like breakfast with Chris was the only option available this morning. How on earth did she manage to go on a breakfast date with Chris? Just her luck.

Parking was never a problem so early on, she had to avoid the trucks and vans at the market, but parking around the corner was free until 7 a.m. She parked up, entered the diner, and saw Chris sitting in front of two huge breakfasts, the world-famous Gut Buster. Chris's was the vegetarian equivalent, but Abi's was a reasonable representation of a future heart attack. She dug in greedily, washing it down with two large mugs of black coffee.

They felt ready for the day. They stood up and headed to Abi's car, Chris had walked in. He didn't have a car. She drove and parked at the station.

Tom's desk was empty, but there were signs of his arrival. Two minutes later he walked to his desk, carrying a large mug of coffee.

"Go grab yourselves one, and I'll see you in the meeting room," Tom picked up his files and walked to the room.

"How can we drink more coffee so soon?" Chris asked, the two mugs were soaking the breakfast in his stomach.

"I think we had better, it's gonna be a long one. Can you grab me one, I need to send a quick text," she smiled at Chris mischievously.

❖

Abi and Chris walked into the room expecting to see Tom sitting alone, but were surprised to see the extra person.

"You know Bob Carver?"

They nodded.

"I think the case is a little more complicated than we first expected, I will explain shortly, so I wanted to bring Bob onboard. Just let him know what you're up to. You'll learn a lot from Bob."

DS Bob Carver acknowledged them. His reputation as an

administrator was well-known across the office. Detectives had spent hours trying to trace files or find names of contacts within a business before going to Bob, who managed to find the details within seconds. He had qualified as a detective eight years before and was rapidly promoted to sergeant, but he never felt suited to the public side of the job, preferring to do research and use his computer skills.

"OK, so let's go through what we know to date," Tom started to note points on the whiteboard. He started with the bullet point, 'Gordon's confession' and then started to write a few points under them, crossing them out as soon as he wrote them.

'Timeline, Anal sex, Hockey'

"I want to go through his confession word by word and prove or disprove every point, especially the timeline," Tom could see Abi wanting to ask a question.

"Go on Abi, spit it out?"

"I must have missed a few things here; what's with the anal sex?"

"It didn't happen. He spun me a line in the interview, and it looks as though he has fiddled with the evidence to back this up and failed. Chris here saw through this one straight away."

Abi looked at Chris, who spoke in a quiet voice, "I'll explain later."

"The thing is, his confession is a pack of lies. We need to pick it apart."

"Maybe he didn't kill his wife?" Bob chimed in with his first point.

A long pause Tom closed his eyes while reflecting.

119

"In all my years, this would be a first. That's for sure. Let's work on the assumption that he did and try to prove otherwise."

"Chris, a quick summary of your conversation with ..," Tom checked his notes, "Carol."

"It's all written up, but in essence, James loved his wife, and she loved him back. Carol was a close friend, and I suspect she would be first to know otherwise. She used to play lacrosse with Sally and a group of others. Although this has ended now, the team still socialises every so often."

"Lacrosse? But we found a hockey stick?" Abi questioned.

"Exactly, you need to work out what was happening here," Tom took over again.

"We also have the initial results from forensics this afternoon, the meeting is booked for noon. I'm sure this will bring up other questions. I met with Gordon again last night, his solicitor wasn't expecting this one; he'd had a few glasses and had to book a taxi to get over."

Chris smiled. Charles Beadle had made an impression on everyone he had met so far.

"I just went through the confession with him again. He repeated this verbatim. It's a script. I can't see him diverging from this script until we confront him with evidence to the contrary. So we have to pick this apart."

"And find him innocent?" Abi's question was impulsive.

"I doubt it, but he is hiding something," Tom stared into space as he spoke. Maybe Abi's question has some merit. This confused him even more.

Another pause for reflection.

"We need to flesh out who James and Sally are. What jobs do they do? Their social life and other contacts."

There was a knock at the door, Tom tried to dismiss them, so they pressed the paper against the glass door. Tom sighed and signalled for them to come in.

"I was expecting this," he said, throwing the Argus at the others. The headline read, 'Police suspect James Gordon of killing his wife Sally'.

Abi and Bob read the front page quickly, the story continued on pages 2, 3, 8 and 9. The article was littered with photographs of James and Sally, with happy smiling faces. Pictures of the house with the 'Police Keep Out' tapes across the driveway.

"Where did they get this from?" Both mouthed the question in unison.

"That was my question last night. There is too much information here for it to be one person on the case; they have a lead from somewhere. But where?"

Abi and Chris looked relieved that he didn't suspect them.

"Anyhow, let's ignore the story for now. Let the Argus go their merry way, and don't let it divert us. Let's flesh out James and Sally for now. Use Bob for any research, the rumours are true. He really is the man!" Tom looked over to Bob who sat proudly.

❖

The message was clear, find out more about James and Sally. Where to start? Thankfully, Bob was able to provide some information within seconds via their LinkedIn profiles.

"It looks like they're a husband and wife team, working for Brunswick Haulage."

"Carol mentioned that when I spoke to her last night," Chris chimed in.

Abi remained silent and returned to her computer, checking her records for the evidence collected from the house in Offham. She found what she was looking for and printed a copy. She walked back from the printer with the document.

"Delivery of goods to Hawksley Enterprises, Skipsea, East Yorkshire. Sixteen pallets of goods, £20,000," she read out the details.

"£20,000? That's an expensive delivery," Bob said, sounding surprised. "Let me do a company search and find out more about Brunswick Haulage."

"Abi, how about you check up on who Sally is and I will focus on James?" Chris suggested a split.

"Cool, I shall start with her friend Carol, do you have her number?"

For just under an hour their corner of the office was silent, yet industrious, as the three of them tried to build up a picture of Brunswick Haulage, Sally and James. LinkedIn and Facebook profiles were viewed and blind searches were made on their names to see if this would uncover any other activity.

James had signed up for a Facebook page just over 5 years before.

Initial updates on golf tournaments and a few shares of amusing golf-related videos dried out after a few months, before the account went inactive. He made no mention of hockey, Chris felt confident in his original suggestion that the hockey stick was not James'.

Sally was the direct opposite on her Facebook page, posting regular updates on her travels, group selfies of her lacrosse friends, and pictures of the children.

Their children, two girls aged 12 and 14, featured regularly in Sally's Facebook posts. They all felt sad for the children at this stage, but thankfully a specialist unit was responsible for their wellbeing. Any questions had to be asked of this unit, which would broach the subject with extreme care. It's sad to lose a parent, but devastating to know the prime suspect was your father. They agreed to keep any questioning of the children to a bare minimum.

"Looks like our man James is a commercial wizard," Bob called out from his computer, signalling the others to come over and see.

"Brunswick Haulage was established nine years ago, the sole director, James Gordon. For six years, it traded modest figures, with a turnover in the region of £200-250k a year and profits around the £30k mark."

Abi was confused, "That doesn't seem like much profit from such a high turnover?"

"Haulage has huge costs. These trucks only do 7-8 mpg, they are most likely leased, or if not leased, they will be subject to a huge loan. It will cost around £30k a year to lease a lorry, insurance can add another £4k a year. Fuel, 8 mpg is around 2 miles per litre. Then you have other operating costs like servicing, liability insurance, tyres, and oil. And at some point, you need to pay the driver. An agency driver will cost you around £30 an hour."

Chris looked impressed, "How come you know so much about the haulage industry?"

"Ever heard of the internet?" Bob smiled. Chris started to colour.

Abi was tapping some numbers into a calculator, "So the trip to Skipsea was a very profitable trip?"

"Yes, exactly. And this I where it starts to get interesting. In the first five years, it turned over £250k a year, with a slight uptick in year six to just over £300k. And the next two years are just shy of £2 million. We don't have any accounts for this year yet."

"Wow!" Chris was impressed.

"Wow, exactly, and the profit margins are considerably higher. Last year, the two directors took over £300,000 in dividends. That's some leap."

"Two directors? Who is the other director?"

"Sally Gordon, the company secretary. She was added three years ago. It's quite a common arrangement, it wouldn't surprise me if she has a limited role in the business. She does sign off on the accounts though."

"And that was Sally's office in the house," as Abi spoke the two looked at her confused.

"The chair was set up low, and Sally was short; I estimate 5' 2" maybe? This was her office. I suspect that she did a bit more than just sign off on the accounts, maybe she was the company's accountant as well? The office was laid out for business. But ..," again the two looked at Abi as she spoke.

"But, there were no files. Two empty drawers, but no files. The computer was also missing," Abi recalled the scene in the office with Bill and Ben.

"But I thought I saw an iMac," Chris seemed confused.

"Nope, that was just a monitor," Abi confirmed the setup.

"And I doubt we will find copies anywhere else, so let's work on the assumption that the files have been disposed of. What else can we go on?" Bob asked the question and pondered the answer.

"Bank accounts can't be disposed of, they should have a list of items in and out," Abi looked at the invoice to Hawksley Enterprises, the payment details showed a sort code and account. How do we get hold of the bank statements?" She looked at Bob for help.

"Leave it to Bob," he smiled.

Around 11.55 a.m. two people walked into the office, Abi looked up and recognised them straight away, Bill and Ben, the forensics team. Tom had booked a room for their update, and he signalled them over to the office. Abi and Chris walked over and joined them. Bob remained, head down, on the computer.

"You've both met Chris and Abi?" Tom asked Bill and Ben and they nodded. "Let's get moving then, what can you tell us?"

Bill turned her laptop screen to the others as a series of photographs backed up her monologue.

"Let's start with Sally." The screen showed Sally's body covered in the bed quilt. "Given the localisation of the blood, we suspect that she died in the same spot where she was hit. The body wasn't moved here. There is a smudge on the seat, we suspect that the body was tilted forward, allowing the blood to drop, and then tilted back. Given the small amount of blood, we doubt that she was moved for long."

The pictures on the screen continued to show Sally from various angles, the once vibrant character was reduced to exhibit A.

"The wound didn't generate too much blood, the coroner should be able to confirm that this is expected from the type of injury."

Chris acknowledged, "The coroner did confirm."

The screen changed to pictures of the hockey stick, the slight smudge of blood just by the curve.

"Now, I'm going out on a limb here. I am not qualified to say and I suggest that you follow this up," Bill breathed in as if to exaggerate her statement, "this is not the murder weapon."

She didn't wait for any response, instead, she continued her monologue.

"First of all, the condition of the stick. It's brand new, it's never been used. We recorded a single set of prints on the handle, those of James Gordon, no prints anywhere else. I don't know what force James would have had to exert to hit Sally with a single fatal blow, but we would expect some bruising of the wood. There is none."

Abi nodded, this was her initial thought.

"And finally, the biggest mystery of all. The blood. Oh, it's Sally's alright, but how did it get there? We are led to believe that Sally was killed by a single blow to her head. If so, how did the blood smudge through so quickly? Maybe a quick splatter of tiny drops, but a smudge? Personally, I don't think a wooden stick has the mass and strength to fracture the skull and kill her. This was not the murder weapon. Your mileage may vary, so don't take my word for it."

Bill had answered quite a few questions in her short statement, but no one present fully believed this was the weapon and felt that it wouldn't take much more investigation to confirm this to be the case. Tom made a note to call the coroner after the meeting.

"Which takes me to the rest of the house. Someone has been busy tidying up their traces," the screen showed various images of where surfaces had been wiped down, the fingerprints smudged. Someone else is involved, and they have been very careful to remove their trace. The screen showed pictures of the glasses in the kitchen.

Two sets of glasses, cutlery, and plates. The first from the dishwasher, the second from the sink. The first set carries fingerprints and DNA from James. The second set washed clean, with nothing of any use available to us.

"And if we continue upstairs, we find the same. This is from the office. The desk surface was wiped clean, as was the filing cabinet. Well, nearly," Bill smiled as she presented the first positive news.

"Nearly. This print was lifted from the inside of the drawer handle. Someone had opened the drawer, and we have a partial print. We have searched the database, but no hits."

The bad news seemed out of place with the continued smile on Bill's face.

The screen changed to the plastic sleeve that Chris had picked up from the bushes and bagged.

"This is the plastic sleeve for a hockey stick. The size and shape are identical to the hockey stick we found under the settee. The one that was not used to kill Sally," Bill emphasised the word not.

"There are four sets of prints one here. One set is from James Gordon, and the second set is from a Derek Stallberg, taken from a drink driving offence two years ago. The final set is unknown. The final set matches the partial print we found on the drawer."

Bill's smile was matched by the others in the room.

"Whoever this fourth set of prints matches has been found both inside the house and on this plastic sleeve."

"And maybe Derek Stallberg works in a sports shop?"

Chris still had the echo of Tom's voice in his ears, 'You'll be surprised just how many crimes hinge on small details like this'. Maybe Tom was right?

"We'll make a detective out of you yet," Tom knew what Chris was thinking.

Bill continued with her narrative, the highlights had been covered, and the rest was mostly a re-tread of the groundwork that led to the initial summary. One point of interest to Abi was the recent prints on the loft hole. Ben had suggested that James may have tried to open this, but excessive paint had sealed the cover.

"And that's about it. You'll have my full report in a couple of days. We have finished with the house now; you might want to do your searches," Bill smiled. There are two types of searches; the delicate fingertip search that the two forensic experts had just undertaken and the 'Bull in the China Shop' search that she knew would follow.

❖

Bill and Ben left the room, and Tom signalled to Bob to join them.

"Thoughts?" Tom asked the single-word question.

"What the fuck?" Chris voiced the words, and Abi's mouth shaped them.

"What the fuck, indeed. We are being spun some lines by Sunny James. I'm not sure what and why."

"I'll explain later," Tom said to Bob who looked confused.

"Abi, you dig into Sally a bit more. Find out who she was. Also, Gordon provided two contacts who he was drinking with in Brighton, can you call them and check the details?" Abi nodded in acknowledgment.

Tom continued, "Chris, see if you can find out who Derek Stallberg is, it may or may not be important. After you've finished, the two of you should head over to Offham. The house is still guarded, but this will end tomorrow morning. I'm going to chat with the coroner. Bob, how are you getting on with the bank statements?"

"Going well, boss. Paperwork completed and signed off. I will approach the bank and hopefully get a download within 1-2 hours," Bob confirmed his progress. The speed at which he navigated these hoops would impress most people, but Tom was used to his efficiency.

"What are you waiting for? Chop chop. Stay here, Bob, I'll bring you up to date."

Chris and Abi left the office and moved to their desks. Bob joined them five minutes later.

"Sandwich?"

"Ooh yes, please. I'll have something meaty and Chris here will probably have roasted lentils on organic spelt wheat bread."

"So ham and cheese, and cheese?" Bob didn't wait for an explanation and knew that the cafe only had two types of sandwiches. Both nodded.

He returned a few minutes later and passed them their sandwiches, both had left a stack of three £1 coins on their desk; he picked them up.

It took around 45 minutes for Chris to trace Derek Stallberg. He didn't have a LinkedIn profile, which might have directed Chris to his place of work. His Facebook profile was scant in detail, the email address registered was a Gmail account, he made a note just in case, and no phone number was listed. In the end, it was just good old-fashioned police work that involved phoning shops one at a time.

He had started with the big chains, Sports Direct and Decathlon, both of which have a presence in Brighton. He then widened the search, looking for smaller shops. After phoning the 15th small shop, he started to despair and then checked his notes. Abi had identified the stick as a Grays GR7000. He called his next shop.

"Hello, I was wondering if you could help me. I am trying to trace Derek Stallberg. Does he work for you?"

"Sorry, no. I'm just a one-man band, no one else works here. Is there anything else I can help you with?"

"Maybe you can, do you know who might sell a Grays GR7000 hockey stick?"

"Grays mostly sells online, but there is a specialist in Burgess Hill, just off the High Street," he provided the details, and Chris jotted them down. "I hope that helps you?"

"That's a great help, thanks so much," Chris hung up the call, searched for the number online, and called.

"Hello, I was wondering if you could help me. I am trying to trace a Derek Stallberg."

"Speaking. How can I help?"

Two minutes later, Chris jumped up and ran to the door.

"See you later. I have a lead."

The bell rang as Chris opened the door. No one was in the store, but he could hear some movement in the backroom. The gentleman walked out.

"Good afternoon. How can I help you?"

Chris held out his warrant card, "Detective Chris Thomas, we spoke earlier."

"Hello detective, I'm Derek. But I think that you have guessed this already?"

"Of course. I am trying to trace the sale of a hockey stick made this

Saturday."

"We sell lots of hockey sticks, detective. We might be a small shop, but most people who come in here know what they want and leave shortly afterward with it. A lot phone ahead to check. Do you have any other details?"

Chris checked his notes again, "A Grays GR7000 hockey stick. Did you sell one of these on Saturday?"

"Ah, the Grays gentleman," Chris looked confused. "Most people come in here with a clear idea of what they want, but late Saturday afternoon, I was due to close 15 minutes later, this gentleman came in asking for a lacrosse stick. He wasn't sure what type, he simply asked for a top-of-the-range stick for a woman. I offered him an STX stick, and then he paused."

Chris listened with interest, the mention of the lacrosse stick stuck out.

"'Better still, can I have a hockey stick?', he asked me. It seemed strange; again, he had no idea of what type, so I offered him the Grays GR7000."

Bingo, thought Chris. "Do you recall what he looked like?"

"Sorry, detective, I'm not one for faces. I was dating the wife for three weeks before I could recognise her," Derek smiled.

Chris's face dropped.

"But there was one thing I do recall; he paid cash. Not many people pay cash these days; instead, he handed over three £50 notes. Long time since I have seen these notes, as I say, hardly anyone pays cash these days. Now, the funny thing, he was wearing driving gloves.

132

On a hot day, he was wearing gloves. He tried to get the notes out of his wallet but couldn't. So he had to take off the gloves to get the notes out. And quite a wad he had too."

Bingo.

"Do you still have the notes?" Chris asked expectantly.

"No, sorry. We normally bank every few days. I don't want £50 notes hanging around, so I dropped off the cash that evening in the bank box."

"I don't suppose that you have any CCTV here do you?"

"We do," Chris's hopes jumped, "but only pointing at the stock. We figured if someone was going to steal something, they would aim for the shelves, so just pointed it there. I don't think that will help you much, will it?"

"You've been a huge help. Thank you so much. One more question: why this shop? If someone wanted a lacrosse or hockey stick, why would they find you? You're pretty tucked away."

"Google AdSense. I wasn't convinced at first. This shop has been around for over 10 years, most people in the sport know us, but when business started to dry up and people went online, we had to find some other way. So we used AdSense. Have you got a phone? Google 'lacrosse sports specialist Sussex'."

Chris picked up the phone and went to the browser. He googled the phrase, and at the top of the list was the shop he was standing in.

"See, it works," Derek smiled.

Chris went to leave the shop as Derek spoke again.

"Is this to do with the murder they reported in the Argus today?"

"I can't say, sir, but I would request that you keep this meeting between you and me. If anyone else asks, please call me at the station," Chris said, passing Derek the card.

Carol had read the news that morning in the Argus and was going through the pages again when Abi called. Desperate for more information, she agreed to allow Abi to visit. Just after 2 p.m., the car pulled up outside of her house, Carol was looking out of the window and opened the door as Abi walked along the path.

"Hello, Carol?" Abi dropped the formalities, suspecting that an informal approach might elicit a better response.

"Yes, Detective Thomson?"

"Just call me Abi."

Carol signalled for her to come in and directed her to the living room.

"Tea or Coffee?"

Abi realised that she was already eight cups into the day, but was conscious that it would be rude to refuse.

"Tea, please, I don't suppose you have herbal or fruit tea?" Abi really couldn't face another coffee so soon.

"I'll take a look."

A few minutes later Carol walked back into the room bearing two cups, and Abi took a sip. It was some herbal concoction that Chris would stock in his flat, 'Quite why anyone would drink this shit', she thought.

"Lovely, thanks so much," she lied.

The Argus paper was open on the floor, and a picture of Sally and her lacrosse friends was on display.

"When was this picture taken?"

Carol looked at the page. "This is a recent one, maybe two or three weeks ago. Looks like the Pelham, we either go there or the Blacksmiths, a tradition started a few years back when we used to play the game."

"You don't play anymore?"

"Not for a couple of years. Situations change, and we don't always have the time to play."

"But the time for a drink?" Abi smiled.

"Yes, that won't change. One week, one of us couldn't make the game but managed to turn up after for drinks. The next week it would be another. We slowly realised that this was a social group; we didn't need to play to be social."

"And Sally always came along?"

"Always. She loved these sessions and always wanted to keep in contact with the group. Well, I say always; she couldn't make it last Thursday, because of work or something, but she did make a meal date with me for Tuesday, tomorrow," the regret that Carol would never see Sally again showed in her eyes as tears formed. Abi noticed and waited a few seconds before continuing,

"Work? Do you know why?"

"She did say something about end-of-year books but didn't give any details."

"Brunswick Haulage? I see Sally worked there with her husband?"

"Yes, that's the one. Although she didn't work with her husband, she did everything from the office at home. James used to bring the paperwork home every evening, and she updated the books and paid the bills. She always said that there wasn't that much to do, but I guess that every business has an end-of-year rush?"

Abi recalled the empty office, no files were present, the computer was missing, and there was no obvious signs of any activity except for the stray invoice behind the desk.

"I guess so. Do you know James?"

"Well, yes. He was her personal chauffeur. He would drop off Sally on Tuesdays and be back a few minutes after she texted him the word 'taxi'. He would sometimes come into the pub for a drink and a chat. He was a nice guy and adored Sally, and she adored him. I can't believe," Carol's eyes misted again, and she struggled not to cry.

"Did Sally change when the company grew?"

"Sally? Change? Not at all. She moved out of the estate, but she had to anyway as the kids were growing up and their flat was tiny. They bought the place in Offham, but she was keen to stay in touch. We used to chat every week on the phone, text most days, and meet on Tuesdays. The only change was we that we split time between the Pelham and the Blacksmiths."

"And the other girls? Have you spoken to them?"

"I phoned two of them this morning, they saw the Argus before I could call them. They are as shocked as I am. Do you really think James killed her?"

"It's an ongoing investigation, and I can't comment at present."

Carol picked up the Argus and said, "But it says here."

"I know what the Argus says, just be assured that no one on the investigation has spoken to the paper apart from telling them what I have told you."

They continued to chat, and Abi was keen to build a picture of the couple. Her tea was gradually going cold; she thought it might be easier to drink colder. As she left, she drank the remains; it tasted no better.

Chris was back at his desk and working as Abi came in.

"Well, that's one mystery cleared, or sort of."

Abi looked at Chris, her eyes asking the question, 'what?'

"James' car. We assumed that the car on the drive was his, turns out they had his and her models, and this was hers."

"And where was James' car?"

"At Cooksbridge station. One of the businesses there allows James to park outside. They saw the Argus this morning and phoned in to mention their car was there. The boss interviewed James, he came out 10 minutes ago and, apparently, he was too pissed to drive after a session in London, so Sally picked him up."

"How is this important," Abi was confused, what was the point?"

"Not important at all. Just managed to tie up one loose end; that's one less to worry about?"

"What did you find out? Spare me the details of anything that's not important."

Chris's mind went back to his training and how small details could be important and how it was key to close them. But Abi had either forgotten the training or simply wasn't interested. He suspected the latter. He thought back to his visit to the sports shop.

"OK, well, I managed to trace Derek Stallberg and also find out where the hockey stick came from."

Abi's eyes lit up at something useful. Chris explained the visit and left the payment until the end.

"So he paid cash and had to remove his gloves?"

"Yes. Matches the suspect, who was careful not to leave prints anywhere. What's the betting he left prints on the plastic wrapper accidentally?"

"Um, yes. What time was he in the shop?'

Chris panicked, the time? He hasn't confirmed the time. A quick phone call would resolve the situation, but then he recalled his notes and how the stranger had arrived 15 minutes before closing. He picked up his phone and googled the store, shop times on Saturdays were 9:00 - 18:00.

"17.45," he said confidently, not admitting that he would need to call later just to confirm.

"So either he went out to buy a murder weapon," she grimaced as she made the suggestion, "or?"

"Or Sally was hit by another weapon prior to this time," Chris jumped in.

"Which means there is another part of James' confession that doesn't add up," Abi completed the sentence.

"What are you kids up to now?" Tom had entered the office, "Let's grab some space."

Chris explained to Tom the purchase of the hockey stick, and the switch from the lacrosse stick and gloves. He also explained the time of the transaction, adding that this was a calculation based on the statement and not a definite time. Tom's look admonished him, and he promised to call and confirm the time.

Abi picked up on the time and her theory that the stick was purchased after Sally had been struck.

Tom sat, thinking for a few seconds before speaking.

"Figures, The pathologist said the blow to the skull was fatal but not necessarily immediate. I will check if she could have been alive for a bit longer."

"The cunt left her to die!" Abi made the statement, It wasn't a question. By her calculation, Sally was alive for 3 hours after the stranger went shopping and was likely hit well before then. They had left her to die for all that time. She made no apologies for her language.

"Seems that way," Tom agreed.

"I called the two numbers that he provided for his company on Saturday," Abi added in her update.

"And?" Tom knew where this was going, but asked all the same.

"Both answered and confirmed they were with James Gordon, and, rather strangely, both explained they were travelling abroad in a few hours. Some yacht show in France or something."

"I don't need to ask, but you traced the phones?" Again Tom knew where this was going.

"Yes. Both were pay-as-you-go devices, purchased a few months ago, and only connected to the network the first time on Saturday evening."

"Burners?" Tom asked the question but made it sound like a statement.

Abi nodded confirmation. She continued, "Yes burners. They barely moved an inch after being turned on. Both triangulated to Osborne Villas in Hove, nothing more specific than that. Once I made my calls, I tried to call the first device again, but it was already turned off. The second as well. Coincidence?"

The three sat in silence for a minute before Tom started to speak again.

Tom broke the silence, "Looks like James' so-called confession is unravelling by the minute. Someone is trying to drag us up the wrong path."

"Are you suggesting that this is a lie? If so, why?" Abi asked the question they were all thinking.

Tom sat thinking and didn't answer. He looked at his watch.

"It's 5 p.m. now. Are you kids OK to pop over to Offham and take a look at the house? Uniform leave tomorrow morning, so let's get a final look before the place becomes contaminated."

They both looked at each other and nodded, turning towards Tom and confirming.

"Look for the not-so-obvious, look for something that's there but shouldn't be or something that's missing. I think you kids call it 'thinking outside the box'?"

Again, they both nodded.

"OK, off you go. See you back here at 8 a.m. tomorrow."

"I'll drive us; there's no need for a pool car," Abi spoke and her head directed them to the exit.

"Two secs, just got to make a quick call," Chris rushed back to his desk and picked up up the phone. Less than two minutes later he walked towards her.

"What was that about?"

"It was 17.45, Derek Stallberg confirmed," Chris was happy both that he had completed the check and been proven right.

As Abi and Chris drove up to the house, Chris noticed Phil. They parked up and walked towards him.

"Which one is Morse and which is Lewis?" Phil called out as they got out of the car. Chris walked over to him, and they greeted each other with a hug. Abi took the more formal approach and shook his hand.

"We go back to police college, both started the same year," Chris noticed Abi's confusion over the greeting.

"We call it a day tomorrow at 6 a.m., but I guess you know that already?" Phil spoke to them both.

"Yes, the boss told us to make one last visit before the place is contaminated. At least we don't need to suit and boot this time."

"In you go then. I'll keep an eye on your car and make sure no one nicks it."

They both walked into the house and took a brief look around, it looked the same as the first time they saw the place, Sally's body was missing, but the blood stain was apparent on the seat cushion.

"Where to start? Are we looking for something missing or something present but out of place?" Abi looked around as she spoke.

"I suggest we start with the loft cover," he walked up the stairs as he spoke.

Standing under the loft cover, he pushed, but the cover didn't give way. He was standing on his tiptoes to reach and was only able to exert pressure with the tips of his fingers. It wouldn't budge. Abi tried, barely reaching.

"I guess neither of us made the basketball team? Let's find something to stand on," Chris was tempted to pull the office chair onto the landing but thought better of it. He went downstairs to the utility room and returned with a step ladder.

"Health and safety requires that you support the ladder," he grinned at Abi who moved to support the ladder as he scaled the first three steps. He pushed, and there was a sharp crack as the paint gave way.

"No one has been up here since the place was decorated, that's for sure."

He climbed up the remaining steps, shone his pen light into the dark space of the loft, found a light switch, and turned this on to illuminate the space, breathing in the cold, dank air.

"Bingo," he said, reaching forward and grabbing the item, passing it down to Abi.

"I guess this is a lacrosse stick?" He was holding the stick in his hand, the net still attached to the end of it.

"Yep, that's a lacrosse stick," Abi confirmed, "Any more up there?"

He looked around the space, which was made up mostly of boxes, "I count three."

Abi passed him the stick, which he replaced, and then stepped down the ladder.

"Looks like he tried to get a stick out of the loft and failed."

"Hence the trip to the shop?" Abi spoke the words as a question but wasn't looking for a response.

They looked around for another two hours and decided to call it a day. Nothing obvious spoke out to them. They were just walking towards the door when Abi spoke.

"Do you play golf?"

"Crazy golf on the seafront, but I suspect this isn't the type you're looking for?"

She ignored the response and walked outside to Phil, asking the same question.

"Now and again. Why do you ask?"

She gestured to Phil to come inside and walked over to the utility room, grabbing the golf bag and emptying out the contents onto the floor. She didn't have a clue what the clubs were, but she ordered them by shape.

"Anything missing?" Her question was directed at Phil.

He stared down at the set and muttered.

"Two Drivers, a 3 wood, a 3 hybrid, 4, 5, two 6, two 7, two 8 and two 9 irons, two pitching wedges, and a putter," he counted out the 17 clubs in front of him, "maybe he doesn't find himself in the bunker that much?"

The other two looked confused.

"He's got all the clubs he needs here and a few duplicates, but he is missing a sand wedge."

Chris googled 'sand wedge' in images and showed the result to Abi who checked the set again.

"Now that would cause the injury," Abi said, and Chris nodded in confirmation. They took pictures of the clubs laid out on the floor and replaced them in the bag, taking a couple of attempts as they didn't quite fit the way they came out.

"While you're here, guys, I have another quandary for you," Phil looked at the two as he spoke. "The picture in the Argus."

Both looked confused.

"It's only been Dave and myself here for the past few days, and neither of us recall the Argus coming out. Once they arrive, they're mostly asking questions and taking shots from all angles, but there's been none of that."

"But someone must have taken a photo? The picture in the paper is obviously recent and has the tape across?"

"Well, there's been plenty of photographers here, that's for sure, but all locals who pull up and grab a couple of snaps on their phone. No journalists, that's for sure."

"Maybe the journalist stopped by, grabbed a few shots, and buggered off?" Chris made his suggestion.

"A journalist stopping by and not quizzing me for 'no comments' for half an hour? That would be a first. Nope, the picture wasn't taken by a journalist, that's for definite."

They bid farewell to Phil, both hugging him as they left. The formal handshake seemed inappropriate to Abi after watching the two men hug. Abi drove along the road and stopped to turn right when she noticed something.

"Ooh, Harveys."

"Ah, yes. I meant to tell you there was a Harveys' pub nearby."

"Would be a shame not to. You OK to drive?" Abi didn't wait for an answer as she indicated to pull into the carpark.

"Hello Chris," Fitz recognised him as he walked into the pub, "on duty today or is this a social call?"

"You're obviously a regular here?" Abi looked at Chris and smiled. She turned her attention to the barman. "We're not on duty, but he'll be driving me home. So I'll have a pint of Harveys and Chris will have a lime soda. Oh, and he's paying. I'm Abi."

"Fitz," he held out his hand to Abi, "good to meet you."

They grabbed their drinks and moved to the sofa by the fireplace. It hadn't been lit for a few months, but the ash was still present in the grate. Abi took a sip and smacked her lips in appreciation.

"The governor will be pleased about the clubs," Chris started to talk about their findings.

"Please," her eyes were directed at the beer, "we're off duty now."

Chris smiled. It had been a long day and there was plenty of opportunity to talk about work in the morning. He sat back and watched Abi relish her beer, she took two big gulps and stood up as she finished the last drops.

"Didn't touch the side. Off to get another one."

She returned and sat down, taking a sip from the glass as she lowered herself into the seat.

"Do you ever switch off from work? How's the dating going?" Abi liked to grill Chris on his love life.

He took a sip of his lime soda, he didn't experience the same joy that Abi did as she sipped her drink.

"Slowly."

"Slowly? You live in Brighton, the gay capital of England, and you say slowly. How much more choice do you want?"

"Some of us are old fashioned in what we want from a relationship. Everyone I talk to wants to get down to it straight away," he blushed as he spoke the words. "There must be a man out there who wants to take it slow, but I can't find him in Brighton."

"How hard are you trying? He must be there somewhere?" Abi pressed Chris.

"Well, two weeks ago, I thought I met him in a bar. We had a long discussion about what we wanted for the future. It was going so well, he walked back with me, and I invited him in for a cup of tea."

"OK, I can see where this is going," she said, taking a sip from her beer grinning.

"What do you mean, you can see where this is going?"

"Let me guess, as soon as you got through the front door ,his hands were all over you and his tongue was down your throat?" Abi didn't wait for an answer, she could see Chris looking back at her, his mouth wide open in shock.

"Look, there are two types of tea. One comes in a cup of brown liquid with milk or lemon, and, well, he assumed you meant the other type," her smile gave way to laughter.

"Look, as I say, it's not that easy."

"And Phil?" The opportunity to ask the question ever since she saw Chris greet Phil at the house earlier.

"Phil?"

"Yes, Phil. Are you going to tell me that you and Phil didn't get it together during training?"

"Phil is a married man - married to a woman - with children," he coloured up as he spoke.

"Yeah, and I date men now. Doesn't mean that I have always dated men, does it?" She lifted the glass to her lips. Clearly, she was enjoying the embarrassment this was bringing Chris.

Chris tried to shape the words with his mouth, but no sound came out. As far as Abi was concerned, she had her answer, whether or not he was going to admit it.

"Well, don't leave it too long. You're getting so boring with work, work, work. You need to get out there."

She looked at Chris, she didn't wait for him to reply. "I'm starving. You?"

He nodded, pleased to hear a change of subject. "Me too."

She jumped up and walked to the bar, returning a couple of minutes later.

"Kitchen closed a few minutes ago, but he says he has some spicy sweet potatoes which we can take away," she picked up her glass and drained the contents. "Off for a pee, let's head straight off so it's hot when we get back."

She stood up and walked to the toilet. Fitz came out with the takeaways in a plastic bag, and Chris was standing waiting when she came back.

"See you again," Fitz waved them goodbye.

Back in 2001 the two separate towns of Brighton and Hove joined to become the City of Brighton and Hove. The locals are proud of their newly joined city but still differentiate between the two halves. When Abi moved into her apartment, she found herself correcting people who spoke of her home as Brighton with 'Hove actually', a term used by the locals for years. The apartment was actually at the far edge of the city, one street away from the town of Portslade, sometimes called West Hove in an attempt to gentrify the area.

It was a small one-bedroom flat with an entrance shared by four other flats. At some point in the past, this was part of a large family home, but, like most of Brighton and Hove, these larger buildings had been reduced to multiple occupancies as the families were replaced by students and singletons.

Abi walked in, kicked off her shoes, and threw herself onto the settee.

"Do the honours, will you? There is a bottle of white in the fridge, you can sleep on the settee if you fancy a glass."

Chris moved into the kitchen space, a room barely big enough for one person to cook. He could see why Abi ate out or had takeaways so often. As he opened the fridge and looked at its paltry contents, he guessed that she had no plans to cook for the foreseeable future.

He had visited Abi's place a number of times, every time it looked cluttered and untidy, yet clean. He could imagine her moving the piles of plates out of the way, cleaning the surfaces and replacing them. There was no other explanation.

He grabbed the wine and two glasses and took them to her, she started to pour. He returned to the kitchen and took two plates from the draining area, dishing the contents onto the plates.

"Cheers," Abi held out the glass for Chris.

"Cheers."

They ate the food in silence, save for a few hiccups, the dish was very spicy, both succumbed.

"Well, that was better than I expected. Maybe there is something in this plant-based food you keep going on about," she mocked him.

"I don't always go on about this. Anyhow, it's got cheese in it, so it's not plant-based."

"Maybe that's why it tastes so good, then?" Abi stood up and grabbed the plates. "More wine?"

She didn't wait for an answer and walked to the kitchen. She walked straight back in, holding the boxes that the food came in.

150

"Well, that's another puzzle solved."

Chris looked confused, "What puzzle?"

"The boxes. We found takeaway boxes at the house and didn't know where they came from. They looked just like these. Obvious, really."

He looked thoughtful for a couple of seconds.

"So why didn't Fitz mention that they came in?" Abi's turn to look confused, Chris continued, "I asked Fitz to ask around if Sally or James had come in, and I'm sure he would have mentioned it."

"Maybe it's the mysterious man with the gloves who bought the takeaway?"

"Who's talking about work now?" Chris taunted her.

"OK, one for the morning then," she said, raising her glass and took a large gulp, Chris sipped his.

He woke to the sensation of Abi shaking his shoulder. The wine was still present in his system, and he felt drunk. Abi was standing by the settee wearing a t-shirt and knickers.

"Sorry mate, you've got to go."

"Uh?"

"Sorry, I forgot I invited Bumble over for breakfast. Won't be quite the same if you're snoring and farting on my settee."

"You could tell him I'm gay?"

"I don't think that'll work. I'll order you an Uber, I can't expect you to pay."

Chris sat up in bed and pulled his jumper over his head, Abi looked at him as if hurrying him along.

"Who the fuck arranges a date for this time in the morning?"

Abi gave him a crafty smile.

Two minutes later, Chris was dressed and herded down the stairs to catch the waiting Uber, while Abi jumped in the shower and quickly sorted herself out for the date.

Chapter Seven

Chris had walked out of Abi's feeling groggy, he had struggled to keep his eyes open on the way home and had just nodded off as the car reached his apartment in Kemptown.

"There we go, mate," the Uber driver said, bringing him back to the world of the awake.

He stumbled out of the car, thanking the driver. He then noticed that he had been dropped off at his old flat, Abi must have provided the wrong details. It was only a short 5-minute walk, but by the time he arrived at the flat and put the key in the door, he was wide awake. He undressed and got into the cold sheets and lay there tossing and turning, unable to resume his sleep.

No point in fighting it, he thought. His previous flatmate had acquired a huge collection of 80s CDs and DVDs before doing a runner, never to be seen again. The intention was to drop them off at the charity shop, but as he started to work his way through the titles, he realised that he had a bit of the 80s in him, even though the 90s were well underway before he was born. He flicked through the titles, an Officer and a Gentleman, Dirty Dancing, he was sorely tempted to watch for, maybe, the 15th time but decided against it. Jagged Edge, never heard of it. Flipped it over and saw Glenn Close and thought of Fatal Attraction, decision made.

Just after 7.30, he was sitting at his desk suffering a mild headache, the result of the three glasses of wine that he had drunk, he wasn't a big drinker, and the disruption to his sleep. He was drinking his second coffee and working his way through a bottle of water. The plan was to get some breakfast as Abi arrived, but as the clock moved rapidly towards 8 o'clock and the scheduled briefing, he realised that this would have to wait.

He opened the case book on his computer and started to enter details of the visit, including the lacrosse sticks in the loft and the golf clubs. He had googled details on a sand wedge and found a picture of one that matched the set of Titleist clubs at the house. The sand wedge didn't look any more of a weapon than the other clubs, suggesting that the choice had been purely random.

"No sign of Abi yet?" Chris hadn't noticed the arrival of Tom, the voice was the first sign he was even in the office. How such a large guy can tiptoe around always amazed him.

"No, sorry. I can text her?"

"Do that, let's get started in 5 minutes."

He quickly entered a text, 'Where the fuck are you?', grabbed his notes, and headed with Bob to the meeting room. Tom was wiping the whiteboard as they entered the room and sat down.

"Here she comes, just on time," Bob and Chris turned their necks to see Abi walking purposefully towards the room, pulling up a chair, and sitting down.

"Good breakfast?" Chris smiled as he whispered to Abi.

"Fuck, yeah!"

"Can we focus, please?"

The two sat like admonished children as Tom started to write on the whiteboard.

Abi held up four fingers, mouthing 'four times,' her face animating exhaustion.

❖

"OK, Day three, Tuesday morning. What do we have to report?" Tom looked at the team and asked for updates.

Bob took the initiative and started to talk.

"Brunswick Haulage is certainly a profitable company. It has grown from a minnow, with a turnover of just over £200k and profits of around £30k, to one turning over millions of pounds in less than 4 years. Turnover has shot through the roof, and so has the profit margin. I have had the company accounts filed for the past 7 years. If we had waited a few days longer, I would have had access to last year's account as well."

The others looked puzzled, and Bob continued in the hope that he could answer their puzzlement.

"The company accounts were due at the end of this month. Sally had previously left the accounts until the last minute, looking at the filing dates for the past 3 years, they were filed within 5 days of the final date."

"Is that unusual?" Abi asked the question they were all thinking about.

"Yes and no. Some companies leave it late because they are disorganised or tardy, others leave it late to pull in as many expenses as possible and reduce the tax bill. It's not illegal, and I suspect over half leave it until the last month, so I don't see anything out of the ordinary, and, as it matches the pattern from the previous two years, I'm not too concerned. The biggest concern for me has been the full

155

books."

"Those that are missing?" Chris spoke for them all.

"Exactly. The accounts filed don't break down to an invoice level. They simply provide totals for the year. Sally has kindly broken these down by month in previous years even though we just need annual numbers. But these don't tell us too much. For example, we can see that they invoiced £430,000 in June, but we don't have a breakdown of where these charges came from. What we need are the actual invoices."

"But we already know, these are missing. Where is this going Bob?" Tom was starting to sound impatient.

"Bob loves to tell a story, believe me, I have heard a few of his in the past, and, looking at his demeanour, I suspect this has a happy ending. But I would love to end this meeting before my retirement kicks in, so can we hurry it along, please?" Tom grinned as he spoke and this brought a smile to their faces.

"OK, boss, deny me my moment, won't you?" Bob joined in with the smiles.

"So we are missing the invoices because the laptop is missing, and so are the paper copies from the filing cabinet. There is nothing of any use at the depot either, they don't keep any filing in that damp and dirty environment. But we have Mr. Jobs to thank for the next bit," Bob said, leading up to the happy ending.

"This is an Apple household. It was an Apple monitor on the desk, Sally and James both wore Apple Watches and carried Apple iPhones. In fact, Sally's watch is with technical now, who will shortly be able to confirm the time of death from the health

156

application."

"But we need the PIN to be able to break these devices, and Apple has strict T&Cs that prevent this?"

"That's right, Chris, Apple is not the best of friends to law enforcement, but thankfully we won't need them. When James was arrested, he handed over his phone and watch and also offered his PIN, he was determined to be as open as possible."

"How is James' PIN going to help us? And how does this help us trace a missing laptop?" Chris looked confused.

"When James offered his PIN he explained that it was his wife's birthday, 0307."

"And the two love birds shared each other's birthdays on their devices?" Tom was grinning. Maybe the story was worth it after all?

"Yes, almost. Sally is a bit more security conscious than James, with a 6 digit PIN, she used the year as well, so we tried 270673, and bingo, we're in."

"OK, so we have her phone, and we can now unlock her watch and see when the heartbeat stopped, how does this help us with the invoices?"

"The iCloud. All of her devices shared the same Apple ID. I can browse all of the files on the iPhone and we have been able to use her Apple id on another laptop, using the iPhone to unlock the password, and we have all the documents. By the time I get back to the desk, I should have close to a thousand documents printed and start to work my way through them."

By this point, everyone was expecting Bob to take a bow; they were all impressed.

❖

Tom looked at the other two, "Aside from a mild hangover and lack of sleep, what have you two managed to find out?"

Chris looked at Abi and signalled for her to take the lead.

"Well, we have two bits of information. I will let Chris do the honours on the second part, but allow me to share mine."

She unlocked her phone and showed them the photo of the food containers on her kitchen side. She had pushed the plates and glasses to one side to keep them out of view, but they could still be seen at the edge of the picture.

"We stopped off at the local on the way home from Offham last night and we ordered a takeaway, these are the containers, and, unless I am wrong, I think you will find that these are the same as those found at the house."

"Another opportunity for you to pop back into the local for a pint?" Tom smiled as he spoke, Abi's reputation for real ale was well known.

"Yes, another opportunity," she grinned, "Someone must have picked up the takeaway, I will pop over there shortly and quiz Fitz. Anyhow, Chris has the best bit of news."

Everyone looked over at a beaming Chris, who was about to talk when there was a knock on the meeting room door.

The person knocking didn't wait for an answer, they strode straight in holding a copy of the Argus, the headline blaring out.

'Offham murder suspect bought the weapon from my store'

The headline was accompanied by a photo of Derek Stallberg in front of the racks of lacrosse sticks. The story went on to describe the model of STX stick sold, matching the evidence found at the house. It also covered details of the purchase, the time of sale, and the fact that it was paid for in cash with £50 notes.

"OK, who the fuck is talking to the press?" Tom's face went from pink, to red to purple in seconds. He had a career of investigations undermined by information provided to the press, and one or two cases lost because of it. All he wanted was the time and silence to investigate, but the public's desire for salacious information, and the press' quest to bring this regardless of the cost to the investigation, made this continually impossible.

Abi and Chris looked horrified that they were even under suspicion, Bob shrugged his non-involvement. Tom looked at all their faces for a long time before deciding they were telling the truth.

"Someone needs to call this Stallberg," he said looking at Chris as he spoke, "and tell him to stop talking to the press."

Chris nodded.

The room remained silent as Tom's face changed colour back to pink at a slower rate than it had hit purple a couple of minutes before.

Chris took the initiative and decided to break the silence.

"I, sorry, we checked the composition of a full set of golf clubs. It's a mixture of drivers, woods, putters, and pitchers."

Tom interrupted, "I do know Chris. I have been playing for years"

"Would you go out without a sand wedge?"

"Without a sand wedge?" Tom looked confused, "The way I play, this is the club I use the most. I have spent more time in the sand on a golf course than I have on the beach."

"Well, Mr. Gordon's golf clubs were missing a sand wedge"

Tom picked up on this straight away, "A golf club would be a lot more effective as a weapon than a wooden lacrosse stick."

"Hockey," Abi tried to correct him.

"Lacrosse stick, hockey stick. Makes no difference. No one believes Sally was killed by a wooden stick. But a golf club would do the damage. Were the clubs dusted?"

"Yes, they were," Abi recalled the telltale signs of dusting for prints on the bag and heads of the clubs.

Tom looked thoughtful, "I think we need to chat with Gordon again. Let's arrange for this afternoon. Abi, you follow up at the pub. Tom, any chance of a summary of the documents for this afternoon? And Chris, give Mr. Stallberg a call and read him the riot act, and then come along with me for the interview."

❖

The phone barely completed its first ring before it was answered.

"It wasn't me, detective," Derek Stallberg answered the call with an immediate apology. He had entered Chris's number onto his phone from the business card he was left with, so he knew who the call was from.

"Sorry?"

"It wasn't me. The article in the Argus, I was planning to call you this morning. I saw the paper on the way to work and have been reading it ever since. It wasn't me, detective. Honest, it wasn't me."

"But it had a picture of you standing by the lacrosse sticks?"

"Promotion picture, look at my website, and you'll see the same picture. And a few more besides, they were taken three years ago. I've still got hair in those pictures."

As he spoke, Chris visited the website and saw the picture of a younger-looking Stallberg beaming at the camera. He compared this to the cropped image on the Argus.

"And you've not spoken to anyone from the Argus?"

"No. I've not even mentioned your visit to my wife, detective. Some people like to gossip, but I don't. This story was written blind."

"Why would anyone do that?" As Chris spoke, he realised that he was thinking aloud.

"Beats me, you're the detective," Stallberg laughed as he spoke the words, so Chris knew it was a lighthearted comment.

"Of course, maybe I should ask one of the other detectives. There are a few of them here. Thanks again, Mr. Stallberg. If you are approached by any journalists, can you be candid? It's a tricky stage of the investigation, and we don't need any theories added to the mix."

"Of course, detective. Have a nice day," Derek hung up as he spoke the words.

Chris still had the phone to his ear nearly 30 seconds after the call had finished, and he stared into space in deep thought.

"Penny for your thoughts?" Tom's voice broke the silence.

"Oh, sorry. Turns out Stallberg didn't talk to the press. The photo is from his website. Someone else had been feeding the Argus the story. Mr. Gordon must have an accomplice."

"My thoughts exactly. Let's go see him now."

The two left the office, taking Tom's car to the custody suite in Hangleton.

"I don't think Gordon killed his wife, but I don't want him to know this. Yet!" Tom had been silent since they got into the car, lost in his thoughts. The words came out slowly, as if planning a chess move.

"Why would he admit it then?"

"Beats me, seems a bit steep to admit to a murder when you didn't do it. He has another plan somewhere, I just can't work it out. I don't think we will get much out of him in the interview, but let's see. You stay silent and keep an eye on him. Look for any twitches or any change of demeanour."

❖

Tom's prediction that he wouldn't get much out of the interview was well-proven. When asked if he wanted his solicitor present, Gordon was quite clear, a definite no. Chris sat motionless, not blinking, staring out James as Tom asked the questions.

"You called the police station at six minutes past midnight."

"No comment."

"I wasn't asking for a comment, I was stating a fact. The call was logged at 00.06."

"No comment."

"Why did you wait until six minutes past midnight to call the police, Sally died sometime before."

"No comment."

"What did you do between killing Sally and calling the Police?"

"No comment."

The questions continued and the responses did not differ, a very determined short sentence was delivered without emotion, "No

163

comment."

"Do you play golf, Mr. Gordon?" Chris's question came out of the blue and surprised both of them.

James hesitated, blinking twice. Both detectives noticed the immediate change in demeanour.

"Sorry, I um, I mean. No comment," his demeanour quickly fixed, he returned to the 'no comment' responses as the questions continued and Chris continued to stare.

James relaxed as he could see Tom's frustration with his responses. He realised that the questioning was coming to an end; a few more neutral responses and he would be led back to his cell to read his book.

"I'm not much of a golfer myself. I play the odd round of crazy golf on the seafront, that's about it. What was it that Twain wrote about Golf?" Chris took up the questions again.

"Golf is a good walk spoiled," Tom replied, looking directly at James as he spoke.

"That's it. A good walk spoiled. Always seems like a strange way to spend an afternoon. I guess that it's also the only way most of these people get a chance to spend time in the sand, as Brighton has a stoney beach"

"It's all down to the clubs. You take a putter into the bunker and you'll be there all week," Tom continued the improvisation, "I forgot my sand wedge one day and went 15 over par on the first three holes. Nearly called it quits before my partner took pity on me and loaned me his. The bastard said he couldn't stop laughing and

164

needed to stop to steady his shot. He went on to win the game, of course."

"Surely you would know if you were missing a club, wouldn't you?"

"Well yes, normally I would. But I was in a rush and threw the clubs in the car, bloody kids had helped themselves to one each."

Tom's gaze didn't change, all the way through the trivial golf conversation, Tom and Chris stared at James. James was unsure who to look at and his eyes moved from one to the other as if watching a game of tennis.

For two minutes the silence remained, James' eyes moving from side to side.

"Did you know that you're missing a sand wedge, Mr. Gordon?" Chris broke the silence.

"Sorry?"

"Did you know that you're missing a sand wedge, Mr. Gordon?"

"Erm, well I. No comment."

Chris referred to his notes.

"Two Drivers, a 3 wood, a 3 hybrid, 4, 5, two 6, two 7, two 8 & two 9 irons, 2 pitching wedges, and a putter."

"No sand wedge," Tom completed the sentence for Chris.

They stared at James, and watched as he swallowed rapidly in an attempt to moisten his mouth.

"No comment."

Tom stared at the clock on the wall.

"The time is 10.57. The interview concludes."

Tom and Chris stood up and walked out of the room. Two minutes later, the guard came into the interview suite and escorted James back to his cell.

❖

It was early, and the pub was closed. It had many doors, and Abi was unsure which one to knock on to get the attention of the landlord. She had parked her car in the carpark and walked around to the front of the building, staring through the window, looking for a sign of activity.

"We open at 11, are you that thirsty?"

Abi looked up at the first-floor window and Fitz leaned out as he called to her.

"On duty, sadly. But if I could have a few minutes of your time, that would be great."

"Pop around the back, I'll let you in." As Fitz spoke, a lorry drove past, blocking out most of his voice. She just heard the word 'back.'

She walked around to the carpark and stared at the building, unsure which door Fitz would come through. The door to the kitchen opened.

"Come inside, detective; how can I help you?"

Abi unlocked her phone and found the picture of the takeaway containers.

"We found a couple of these containers at Mr. Gordon's house, they look like the type of containers you would use."

Fitz was handed the phone, and he studied the photo for a few seconds.

"Yes, they could be ours. Pretty standard containers, though, I don't doubt that you would get the same answer from most pubs around here. But they could be, yes."

"Do you recall Sally or James coming in to collect food on Saturday?"

"I had the evening off and went to watch a band at the Komedia, but my wife was on shift; I'll call her," he stood up and walked to the stairs and called her.

"She should be down in a minute or so," Fitz walked over to the appointment book and looked under the takeaway section for Saturday.

"We've got a few orders that evening," he scanned through the names, "here you go."

Fitz pointed to the order as he passed the book to Abi.

"Hello," Debbie said as she walked in to see Fitz chatting with Abi. It was more like a question than a greeting.

"Hello, I'm Detective Thomson. I'm investigating the murder in Offham. I understand that Sally Gordon collected a takeaway on Saturday?"

"Hello, Detective. Yes, Sally did order a takeaway, but she didn't collect it. We called Sally and her husband answered. Someone else came in to collect it, around 7 p.m. I never met him before."

"Can you describe him?"

Debbie stood in silence, looking at the ceiling, as she tried to recall the event.

"I can't describe him as such, but I recall he was wearing a casual jacket and a cravat. And he was wearing driving gloves, not many people do that these days, so it kind of stuck out."

"Old, young?"

"I would say 50's, just a guess. He came in, paid and took the takeaway. I didn't talk to him."

"Did he pay cash or card?"

"Do you realise how many customers we get on a Saturday? I'm not sure."

"Detective, we will be happy to provide details of the cards used that evening if that's any help?" said Fritz.

"We're both fond of Sally and her gang, they would come in here most weeks and sit by the fire having a jolly time," he said, pointing to the same seats where Abi had sat the night before.

"Anything we can do to help, detective," Debbie spoke.

"Thank you. If you could get the card payments, we can check them out."

"It'll take a couple of hours or so to go through the receipts, can you come back and collect?"

"Sure."

"Another thing. I don't know if it's important, but I recall that he came through the front door and left through the back door. Maybe he didn't realise we had a back door, so parked and walked around. Probably nothing, but I thought that I would mention it."

Abi made some notes.

"Thanks, you've been very helpful. I'll pop back later this afternoon, if that's ok?"

"No problem."

Abi stood up and moved outside to the carpark, through the same door she had come in. She walked to her car and sat inside, looking at the back door. It wasn't exactly hidden, and a back door to a pub is far from unusual. Why would this mystery guy come through the front door?

She got out of the car and started to walk to the front again. A footpath to her right, along the front of the pub, to the left, the footpath ended. She turned right and walked, with the Norman church and the road leading to Offham to her left. The paved path abruptly came to an end where a chalk path came down from the Downs. She turned right along the chalk path.

The path started flat but gradually got steeper, she could hear a call in the distance.

"Millie, Mille!"

A very excited cockapoo came running down the path, and she bent down to greet it.

"You must be Mille?"

The dog responded to her voice and wagged its tail as she stroked his head, grabbing the collar as she knew it was close to the main road.

"There you are, Millie. Thanks so much," the lady said as she slowed as she came down the path, realising her dog was safe. She clipped the lead on the collar.

"Thanks again"

"No problem, Millie is a lovely doggie."

The owner walked off with Millie, her tail wagging.

As Abi stood up she looked at the large object beside her. She was trying to make out what it was. It looked like a large piece of machinery that would fasten to the front of a tractor. It must have been left there a decade ago. Maybe forgotten? Maybe discarded?

The rust had eaten away most of the structure, but the shape remained, with a couple of rusty chains dangling from the top. Nature had gradually encompassed it, a couple more years and it would be totally covered just as the rust finally caused the structure to collapse under its own weight.

The countryside is covered in old, discarded farm equipment like this, wrapped in vegetation, too expensive to clear and just left to rot.

As she stared at the object, imagining the farmer leaving it there one day and not realising it would never be used again, she noticed the glint of a shiny object just to the right. The contrast between the dull rust and the chrome of the object caught her eye. She leaned forward trying to reach it - maybe a bit too far. She took a couple of steps into the undergrowth and reached out again.

In the hedge was a discarded carrier bag marked 'Safeways', the plastic had survived a lot longer than the now-defunct business. Wrapping the bag around her hand, she picked up the object. She noticed the marking and turned it into the light to read the word.

"Titelist. I don't know anything about golf, but I'm willing to bet you're a sand wedge," her words were spoken to the inanimate object.

She walked to her car, the golf club wrapped in the plastic bag.

"Good work," Tom said, listening to Abi's report on the golf club she found. He was impressed by her curiosity and intuition, great characteristics for detectives.

Tom was also pleased by Chris in the interview room, although he had requested he remain silent, the sudden, and random, questions had shown a dent in James' defence. His mobile phone pinged.

Tom read the message aloud, "James Gordon requested a meeting with his solicitor two minutes after you left."

"Something's rattled him," Chris smiled as he spoke.

"Maybe the thought of not returning to the golf course for some time has worried him?" Bob chuckled as he spoke the words.

"Come on, Bob, you're sitting there smiling like a Cheshire Cat. What have you got for us? Are you going to give me the third bit of good news today?" Tom directed Bob to give a summary.

"The invoices are an absolute gold mine of information. It will take a few days to work my way through these, but the story is starting to tell itself," he paused for dramatic effect, Tom was right, he loved to tell a story.

"How does a business grow overnight to this scale? And, why did it grow so quickly and then seemingly stay that size? Talk to any businessman, and they will tell you that you have to constantly innovate, you can't sit back and expect the work to just keep on coming in?"

"But I assume that Brunswick Haulage has managed that?"

"Yep. It grows from around £200k to over £2 million in a year and stays there. Did Gordon run out of ambition? Did he, as they say, rest on his laurels, and the money kept on flowing in?"

"But what do the invoices tell you? We knew the business had grown phenomenally and stayed there before you had access, what have you learned?" Tom wanted to get to the meat of the story, he didn't need Bob's grand introductions.

Bob had printed three copies of two invoices. He passed the copies to them.

"Invoice dated June 2015, delivery of 14 pallets to Cave Castle, South Cave. Total cost, £650. South Cave is a small town in East Yorkshire. Second invoice, dated June 2019, 16 pallets to Skipsea, East Yorkshire. This is the invoice you found behind the desk, Abi."

Abi studied the two items side by side, and she looked up both towns on the maps application on her mobile phone, they were 30 miles apart.

"Wow! 14 pallets for £650 in 2015 and 16 pallets in 2019 for £20k. That's some inflation!"

"Indeed, and I have found a few others that can be compared."

"But where does this leave us? No law prevents a company from overcharging for their services?"

"I agree, that's what I need to work on. There is a lot more to do, I'll get there. For now, I am looking at hundreds of sheets of paper that would stink less if they were made from manure," Bob paused; he was unsure.

"Spit it out, man, spit it out," Tom knew from years of working with Bob that he never presented a theory unless he had the evidence to back it up.

"OK, it's just a hunch, and I am far from proving it. But I think that Sally uncovered something in the books that resulted in her murder. It's just a theory, so don't quote me on this. Give me the space, and I will give you the evidence."

"OK, Bob. You've got the space, and," he looked first to Chris and then to Abi, "you roll up your sleeves and work on this with Bob. Let's split the work and get this done."

Both nodded, neither relished the thought of working through reams of information, but both suspected there was gold to be found.

"Thanks, boss, I also got the bank statements through today. I need someone to consolidate the receipts and outgoings."

"Receipts? I thought we'd lost all of the paperwork?" Abi looked puzzled.

"As I said, Sally was the dream bookkeeper. She wanted a nice, neat filing system, so she would sellotape all of the receipts onto A4 sheets and then scan them. We have managed to download six years of company records from iCloud. What a shame she didn't get an iPhone earlier," Bob's Cheshire Cat smile made even more sense as he spoke the words.

❖

The meeting broke up. Tom and Bob headed to their desks. Abi and Chris checked their watches, looked up, and spoke at the same time.

"Lunch?"

They both nodded their acceptance and walked out into the sunshine.

Like a lot of cafes in Brighton, the Redroaster started life as a simple, straightforward cafe that was reasonably priced, but as the demographics of the city changed, especially in Kemptown, from small families to childless professionals, the cafe went upmarket. As a local and childless professional, Chris loved the place.

"Fuck me. Is there anything affordable on this menu? We're only coppers."

Chris smiled, it was the same reaction every time unless, of course, the establishment sold real ale.

"It's nourishing, and it's close to the office, we have to be back there soon."

"I am starving, I haven't eaten since last night."

"I thought you invited a friend over for breakfast," Chris emphasised the word 'breakfast' using finger quotes, "I imagine you would have served him the full English?"

Abi grinned back, she didn't do embarrassment in Chris's company.

"I thought you ate four times," Chris again chose to emphasise 'four times'.

"No time to eat," she grinned.

The waiter came over just as Chris was trying to dig deeper.

"Three brunches, please. One veggie, and two with meat, and two Americanos, black," she folded the menu as she spoke and picked up Chris', offering him no option to speak for himself.

The waiter looked at Chris.

"Yes, as she said."

The waiter walked away.

"So, are you seeing Bumble again?"

"I've invited him for breakfast again tomorrow. It works best for both of us, who knows what time we will finish tonight? And that," she looked at Chris firmly, "is not an opportunity to talk shop."

"Who wants to talk shop? Tell me more about Bumble, sounds a lot more interesting to me."

Bob had produced two piles of paperwork for when they returned from lunch. One was a copy of invoices, and the other copies were receipts and bank statements. These were duplicates of the documents he was working on. He deliberately didn't provide any instructions, as he wanted a different approach to see how the results compared. Abi picked up the invoices, and Chris the receipts and statements. Both returned to their desks and, without conferring, loaded Excel on their PCs.

The first success came from Chris within 30 minutes, he wandered over to Bob's desk with a couple of the receipts.

"You know you were praising Sally for copying all of the receipts on A4 paper and then scanning them in?"

Bob nodded.

"Take a look. I don't think this is her work."

He passed the two documents, on both examples there was a smudge along the edge. Bob looked closer.

"An oily fingerprint?"

"I think so," Chris confirmed.

He continued, "I don't think Sally was the messy type, maybe these receipts were photocopied in a different location? Somewhere a little less clean?"

"Like a portacabin in the lorry yard?"

"Exactly."

"Good work, Chris. Make a note of those with the smudges and see if there's a pattern."

Chris walked back to his desk, feeling smug.

The second success took a little longer, but was equally important.

176

Abi started to research the companies involved in the delivery, a few had recently gone under, so the information on these was limited, but most of the remaining ones had a website describing their business model. The initial idea came from the two invoices Bob had presented at the start of the discussion. Hawksley Enterprises, the car workshop in Skipsea, had ceased trading, so there was little to be gleaned online.

Cave Castle was still trading and, judging from the website, was doing pretty well. As a test, she called the hotel and asked for availability for weddings and was told nothing was available for 18 months, unless she wanted a midweek wedding. This was clearly a viable business. The 14 pallets were probably fine wines, they had quite a range on their website. £650 seemed a sensible cost for that type of delivery.

She started to check out the other businesses. She found a paint warehouse in the Midlands that received 12 pallets at a cost of £15k; a pet store warehouse that took 6 pallets for £9.5k; a Scottish brewery (they advertised their products as brewed with locally sourced ingredients) 10 pallets at £8k and a small DIY store in Scarborough that took delivery of 4 pallets for £4k. She was intrigued by the Scottish brewer, so she called them.

Ten minutes later, she put the phone down. Even she had to admit that most of the call was spent talking about the brewing process and the range of beers. She knew, before she asked the question on the delivery, what the answer would be, the focus on local produce was key to the business, the hops they used travelled the furthest, and that was only 20 miles.

"Brunswick Haulage? Never heard of them."

"They're a haulage company in the South of England."

"What would we be needing from England?"

"What about your equipment? Where did it come from?"

"It was here before I was born, lassie."

She finished the call by promising to visit one day, and she meant it. She called the DIY store in Scarborough, a family run business operating from a small shop with tins stacked to the ceiling, the type of place that would struggle to store the contents of four pallets, let alone be rich enough to pay £4k for the delivery. She quickly realised that most, if not all, of the deliveries were bogus.

So she turned her focus to the companies that no longer existed. When a company goes bust, they must appoint an administrator to tidy up the company and close it down, if there are no funds available, then the authorities will appoint a receiver to wind things up. A register of companies under administration is available online. She checked the first four companies on the list and was able to derive the type of business and the date that it collapsed.

"Do you have a minute?" Abi had wandered over to Bob's desk. His paperwork was sorted into piles, both on the desk and all over the floor area by his desk.

"Whats up?"

She showed him the four invoices from the failed companies.

"Seems like Brunswick Haulage was the kiss of death for these. Fru's Records, delivery in May 2018, went bust in August 2018. Capstan Boats, delivered in February 2017, went bust four months later."

She held up the other two invoices.

"I suppose you're going to tell me these suffered the same result?" Bob didn't seem surprised.

"Yup, both started to wind up within four months. These are just those who have gone bust. I have spoken to a family run business in Scarborough who would go bust if they paid the delivery and a Scottish brewery who have never taken delivery of anything outside of their own post code in decades."

"Have you found any invoices that make sense?"

"Just the one, the Cave Castle invoice you showed us earlier."

"Well I have a few more," Bob leaned down and picked up the papers from one of the smaller piles. "Take a look."

She picked up the small pile and flicked through them.

"Not their most profitable work."

"Exactly. I started off this pile for any invoice lower than £2k and then started to check, all seem viable businesses and, with a few exceptions, are still trading. Most of them have been loyal customers for as far as the invoices go back."

"Wow. It's that blatant?"

"Yep. And if Sally hadn't backed up to the iCloud, we would be none the wiser."

"Bob had packed his stack of paperwork at 6 p.m. and quietly left the office. Both Abi and Chris nodded as he left. An hour later, Tom walked out and suggested they do the same. Both nodded again. The next time they looked at the clock, it was past 8 p.m.

"Time to go home, partner," Abi had packed her stack of papers, all labelled and stored in her desk.

"Come on, I'll give you a hand to pack away, let's call it a day and grab a drink."

Chris looked up at Abi as she gave her 'resistance is futile' look. He quietly acknowledged her and started to pack up.

"Let's pop in and see Fitz, we need to pick up some receipts."

"And I suppose I'm driving you back afterwards?" Chris looked resigned to his role whenever beer was involved.

"You got it."

They left the office and went to the carpark to collect her car. Soon they were driving along the A27 towards Lewes.

"By the way, I've got you a date," Abi said matter-of-factly.

"What the fuck are you on about?"

"Bumble. His friend is gay and is looking for a partner, he is old fashioned, or boring, as I call it, and I suggested you to him?"

"You managed to get into an in-depth discussion about my relationship needs in-between the four trysts you had with Bumble for breakfast? Go on, tell me how this happens. How on earth did you come to be talking about me?" Chris was looking over at Abi as she was driving, her eyes focused on the road, her grin wide and beaming at Chris's discomfort.

"He saw you leave. I had to explain to him why a man was leaving my apartment at 4 a.m.; some people are suspicious, you know."

"He saw me leave? You said you were jumping into the shower right after I left. It didn't give you much time to prepare breakfast," Chris stressed the phrase 'prepare breakfast' as he spoke.

"Very little time. He buzzed the door, so I told him that I would be in the shower and invited him to join me."

Chris looked shocked. "Sometimes you amaze me, I don't know why, but you do."

"Greetings detectives. Is this official or social?" Fitz called out.

"If you can give us the receipts, then we can conclude the official business and get down to the social," Abi returned his smile as she spoke.

"Well, I can save you time on the receipts. Apart from a couple of beer sales of less than £10, no one paid by card between 6.30 and 7.30, so it must have been a cash sale. I can show you the receipts if you want?"

"No, that will be fine. A cash sale, it must have been. Official business is over; a pint of Best and a lime and soda for my driver, please."

Chris had already walked over to the seat by the fireplace, the same seat that Sally used to share with her friends. Abi walked over, sipping the beer as she did. She passed him the lime and soda.

"So, shall we make it a double date?"

"What? Can you stop talking about my private life, please? Anyhow, I doubt the friend is even interested."

"He is."

"What? He has asked him already?"

"Yup," she said, taking a sip of her beer, licking her lips. She was relishing this moment. "I sent him your photo today, and he came back to say yes."

"My photo? When did you take it?"

"Doesn't matter. The key thing is that he said yes, and he knows that he's not getting any dick for a few weeks, so your type of man," she handed her phone with the picture of Chris's date.

"Sometimes you just amaze me," he looked at the picture, and his face lit up.

"So, that's a yes?"

"OK, yes."

❖

Chris showed an interest in his future date and, not wanting to appear to be obsessed before even meeting him, continued to ask Abi questions throughout the evening. She answered every question, despite knowing as much about the date as he did, keen to keep him interested.

Fitz called time and Abi rushed to the bar for a final pint. She drunk this rapidly and they both left via the rear entrance, passing Chris her keys as they walked towards the car.

They drove through Lewes and onto the A27 just as the fuel light came on.

"Looks like you need a top up," Chris gestured with his eyes looking down at the dials.

"There's an all-nighter by the Vogue. Do you mind stopping there and I'll fill up?"

"Always here too serve, m'lady."

They pulled into the service station and Abi jumped out and started to fill the tank. While he waited, Chris's eyes moved to the pump and the available means of payment. He recognised symbols for Visa, MasterCard and American Express The other payment methods he was unsure of, AllStar, Key Fuels, dieselAdvance, fastFuel and Wex. To the average trucker or van driver these brands are probably as well known as the brands of golf clubs are to golfers. He mused about how we live in our own little bubble and are not aware of the things that impact others in their bubble.

"Wakey, wakey," Abi's voice accompanied the blast of warm air as the door was opened.

"Uh?" He came out of his stupor.

"Are you OK with dropping me off and then leaving the car at the station tonight?"

"OK, as long as you're OK with me walking the mile or so from the station to my apartment?"

"Works for me."

They drove to the seafront and along to Hove, mostly in silence. It had been a long day for both of them and both were keen to rest, especially Abi who had to get up for her early breakfast.

"See you at 8," Abi said as she closed the door, not expecting a reply.

He checked his mirror and turned the car around, heading back to Brighton along the seafront. Tuesday wasn't the busiest of nights in Brighton, but the warm night had brought out a decent crowd. He pulled up at the traffic lights by the Brighton Centre and looked up at the police presence on East Street. The atmosphere was calm and friendly, but he was well aware of how quickly this could change from his early days in training. He didn't envy the police on the beat trying to keep the peace.

He parked up Abi's car and walked out of the carpark, cutting down a side street to Edward Street and walking along as it turned into Eastern Road.

Just before Sussex Gardens, he stopped at the petrol station and ordered a Mars Bar and a can of Coke through the nighttime window. The attendant went into the shopping area to collect the items. As he waited, he found himself looking at the list of payment methods on the window.

His apartment was a short ten minute walk from the petrol station, within two minutes of opening his door, he had undressed and crawled into bed, falling into a dreamy sleep after directing Alexa to wake him at 6.30 a.m.

Chapter Eight

At 4 a.m. Chris's dreams had taken him back to the petrol station, where he found himself looking at the fuel cards, each with a logo presented in a credit card shaped box.

It's strange how the logo is everything for organisations and companies these days. The Sussex Police logo was present all around the office and was protected by copyright, a page on the main website directed third parties on how the brand should be used. Woe betide the business that used the logo to promote the fact that coppers ate their sandwiches there.

He woke up, grabbed his phone and started a Google search.

Every card a unique logo, the Visa one was the word in blue with an orange flash on the V and the Mastercard was two overlapping and interleaved circles, one red and one orange, with the name written through the middle. These were posted on the doors of every retail outlet across the land and were instantly recognisable.

The fuel card logos were new to him, the Esso and Shell cards used their respective and well-recognised corporate logos, the allstar image was the word written in black across an orange background, with an orange star at the top right, dieseladvance had the outline of a crescent under the words.

He quickly showered, dressed and headed to the office.

At 5 a.m., just as Bumble was reading the post-it note on Abi's door, Chris was back at his desk.

As he'd ploughed through the receipts the previous day, Chris had transcribed the amounts into a spreadsheet, one row for each item, adding the date, the payee and a description. As he added more items, he realised that he should categorise the items (fuel, servicing, parts, subsistence, etc.), adding another column which required him to go back through the previous receipts to work out this information. He was left with an impressive looking document, but he wasn't quite sure what he was looking at. Data is nothing without context.

He was now sitting at his desk, going through the receipts again and adding items to a new column, the payment method. Some of the items were on account, such as servicing costs paid direct to the garage. Given the amounts involved, fuel was paid by card. The company used two cards, one was a corporate Visa card and the other was the allstar fuel card. On a single instance cash where was used, he suspected the driver had lost or forgotten the card.

By 8 a.m. he had entered most of the details on the spreadsheet, but still didn't know what he was looking for. Why did he feel compelled to leave his warm bed so early to enter information that meant nothing?

Abi has brought him coffee, she placed this down among the numerous empty cups that sat by his computer monitor.

"Morning partner. What time did you get in?"

"Oh," he looked up at the beaming Abi, "Not sure. I had a hunch about something, but I can't make sense of it. It'll need a bit longer."

"Anything I can help you with?"

"Maybe, let me ponder for a while. How was breakfast?"

Abi smiled, her smile in total contrast to Tom's who was walking purposefully over towards them with a face that had turned purple. He signalled to both of them to enter the meeting room, he was clearly too annoyed to use words.

❖

As they walked into the room, Tom slammed the copy of the Argus on the desk. The headline was screaming out at them.

"James Gordon didn't kill his wife."

They both looked at the front page, skimming the words and taking in the gist of the story, Abi turned the page on an unstated signal, and they continued to read. They finished reading and looked up.

"There is something dodgy going on here."

Bob walked into the office as Tom spoke, he continued.

"The story claims that Gordon is innocent. It says the supposed murder weapon couldn't have been used, stating that another weapon was used, perhaps a golf club. I could go on."

"It's well informed, but not that informed. It hasn't mentioned we have the golf club, so this definitely isn't sourced from within the station," Abi could see Tom relax as she spoke.

"Fuck me. Yes, this is definitely not sourced from within the station, not that I ever doubted you. I bet there are a few other holes in the story as well. Pass me the paper."

The four of them read the pages together, Chris and Abi reading upside down, trying to read the detail. Tom grabbed a Sharpie and started to write on the whiteboard.

Weapon recovered.

Doesn't list the club type.

No mention of the documents we have recovered.

"Anything else?"

"They have repeated Stallberg's claims from yesterday, he was adamant he didn't make a statement to the paper," Chris added.

"Time of death is reported as 19.15," Abi commented.

"But that's correct, isn't it Bob?" Tom looked over as he asked the question.

"Spot on, read the report from the iWatch this morning. It says 19.17, but 19.15 is close enough."

"I was asking for discrepancies Abi, why do you mention this?"

"Because it is so accurate. We had guessed the time up until now, around the 19:00-20:00 mark, I didn't know Bob had the exact time until just now. How can they be so accurate?"

"The accomplice?" Tom stated what they were all thinking.

"So the accomplice is feeding the information. Why would they do this? What is to be gained?" Abi wasn't expecting any quick answers, she just wanted to put the question out there.

Tom's phone buzzed and he looked at the message on the screen.

"Matey's solicitor has requested an urgent meeting. My hunch is we are just about to find out. Chris, you come along with me."

"Can you take Abi? I'm working on something, I would appreciate the space."

"I saw your coffee cups earlier, you've been here for some time?"

Chris nodded.

"Ok, Abi, let's go."

Tom and Abi walked out of the meeting room, Chris and Bob lingered.

"You want to go through anything with me?" Bob detected his confusion.

Chris nodded.

Abi carefully unwrapped the two cassette tapes and placed them in the drawer. She closed both together with a solid click. Since arriving in the room with the waiting James Gordon and his solicitor, no one had spoken and a simple nod was the only acknowledgment.

"Coffee?" Abi looked at Tom, the question was for him and him only. If Gordon and his solicitor wanted a drink, they would have to ask.

Tom acknowledged and Abi left the office. Tom remained silent, looking down at his notes and deliberately ignoring the other two, a skill he had developed over the years. A few minutes later Abi came in with two plastic cups of a brown liquid, she assumed they were coffee as this was the button she had pressed on the vending machine. She looked at the clock on the wall, the time was 10.28 and a few seconds. She watched as the second hand tracked around the clock until it was 10.30. She pressed the record button on the tape recorder.

"It's 10.30 on Wednesday 1ˢᵗ July, present are Detective Constable Thomson and Detective Inspector Christoper. We are interviewing the suspect, James Gordon. His solicitor Charles Beadle, representing," the opening words were perfunctory and a legal requirement.

"I must remind you, James Gordon, that you are still under oath. Would you like me to repeat the oath or are you clear on the requirements?"

James nodded.

"For the record, James Gordon has nodded his consent," Abi spoke to the microphone.

"You asked to meet us, gentlemen. What would you like to say?" Tom took control, looking into Charles' eyes as he spoke.

Charles coughed, clearing his throat and stared at him for a few seconds, he wanted to capture the expression on Tom's face as he spoke.

"Detective inspector, you have held my client for four days now on these trumped up charges of murder. When my client is presented to the magistrate tomorrow, he will be plead not guilty and I will request that he be bailed."

Charles achieved the response he was looking for, despite Tom's best efforts to contain himself.

Tom tried to remain unflustered, but he could feel his face colouring and the anger rising from his stomach. He knew that any response now would expose his feelings, so he remained silent. As they had driven to the interview suite, Tom had requested Abi hold her cool as well. He was expecting some response like this following the Argus report, maybe not so direct and instant, but a response all the same. Both remained silent.

"As the Argus so kindly points out today, your case against my client has no evidence, short of a confession that was obtained within hours of the brutal killing of his wife. He was clearly distressed, and the words he spoke cannot be taken as evidence unless corroborated. What evidence do you have on my client, Detective Inspector?"

Tom remained silent, he could sense the colour in his face subside and the initial heat from his anger replaced by a cold sweat. Let him talk, let him talk.

"First of all, you don't have a murder weapon. You have a report that someone, as yet unknown, purchased a hockey stick, which was found at the scene, but you know this can't be the weapon. You have not identified a motive. Should I go on?"

Tom continued to stare at him, not even blinking. Yes, go on he was thinking.

"None of my client's so called confession makes any sense. He was clearly shocked at what had happened and this came out in the interviews. What evidence do you have?"

"Sir, we have a dead body that has been identified as Sally Gordon. Your client called to say he had murdered her, when we arrived on the scene, he was sat, calmly, in front of his dead wife," Tom could not stay silent any longer.

"We are not disputing this event, my client was indeed present at the house when your officers arrived, and it was his voice on the recording, but you have no proof that he did it."

Charles looked at Tom, attempting to outstare him, but Tom was an expert in this. Charles eventually broke.

"As I say, Detective Inspector, I shall request that the magistrate bail my client unless, of course, you can present evidence that will stand up in court. I shall now request that we call an end to this interview, unless you want to discuss anything further?"

Tom looked at the clock, "Interview ended at 10.47." He signalled to Abi, who pressed the buttons on the tape deck, ending the recording.

No further words were spoken, Tom exited the room. Abi hung back as Charles also left and the guard came through to collect James.

"Money laundering is a process that criminals use to make it look like the money they have is legitimately earned. What they're doing is taking 'dirty money' and effectively 'cleaning' it," Bob was answering Chris's rhetorical question, reading the answer directly from Google.

"I think that Brunswick Haulage is a front for a money laundering scheme," Chris made his positioning statement.

"Go on," Bob said not disagreeing.

"None of the trips, sorry, very few of the trips, make commercial sense to the company commissioning them. Maybe one of two love the service provided, not that there is any sign of any USP. Eddie Stobbart make their drivers wear a tie, but Brunswick offers nothing unusual"

"Edeeeeeeeeee!"

"What?"

"Oh, I forgot you're so young. A few years back, it was the norm to yell 'Edeeeeeee' as an Eddie Stobbart lorry went by and people used to collect truck registration plates like train spotters collect train numbers," Bob tried to explain the short lived craze to a confused Chris.

"You really are a fountain of knowledge," Chris smiled as he spoke. Always good to break the tension.

"Brunswick is clearly not a Stobbart operation, is it? They collect pallets and deliver them, just like hundreds, maybe thousands, of other hauliers around the country, yet they can charge maybe ten times the price for the effort. It doesn't make sense, does it?"

"Ok, we're agreed. But where is the laundering? What have you found?"

"I have been looking at the fuel bills. Most of these are via the allstar card"

"A common form of payment for fuel these days. Most garages take allstar and large fleets can save up to 10 pence a litre at the pump. I can read these details on the internet as well as you Chris, tell me something I don't know."

"Most is via allstar, but a small amount is via the company Visa credit card. Do you remember how we identified a small number of seemingly valid deliveries, where the charges reflected the job?"

"Yes, I recall it well. It seems like only yesterday I was explaining the same to you," Bob smiled, in some investigations people forget who discovered a link. As it was only the day before he didn't want to lose.the praise for this small breakthrough so soon.

"I will rephrase, yesterday you identified a small number of legitimate deliveries," Chris looked to Bob who nodded his approval of Chris's belated recognition. "Well, all of these deliveries are linked to the Visa card."

"Oooooooh, carry on," Bob sat upright, Chris was on to something.

"Well, that is all I have found so far," He looked at Bob who slumped back in his seat. "But, it does beg the question 'why?' and this is what I am trying to work on."

Chris turned the computer monitor so that both could see the detail he had collected.

"What am I missing?" Again, a rhetorical question was asked to the ether in the hope of some divine inspiration.

"Here's an idea, apply for a card and see if that answers any questions? Forward me a copy of the spreadsheet and I will see what else is missing."

"Well, every day is a new day for me and something comes along to amaze me. Mr. Gordon is planning to plead not guilty when we take him to see the magistrate tomorrow, and, get this, his solicitor is applying for bail and expects to get it," Tom had called a quick team briefing as soon as he got back to the office.

"But we have his confession," Chris looked gobsmacked at the news.

"We have his uncorroborated confession. What has he told us, save the fact his wife is dead, that we can substantiate?" Tom was initiating a game of devil's advocate.

"We have the murder weapon," Abi chimed in.

"We have a potential murder weapon. All we know for sure is that this matches the missing golf club and Gordon's prints confirm this. There is no blood on the club, and it could have been disposed of or lost long before."

"But we know that the mysterious person with driving gloves came in through the front door and could have disposed of the club then," Abi persisted.

"Could have. All circumstantial evidence, will be torn down by a lawyer within minutes."

"We have Gordon's sperm on the victim?" Chris responded.

"They were married, sex between married partners is not that uncommon and, as he made clear, it was his birthday, so even less surprising," Tom was deflecting every response with ease.

Abi contemplated a future where sex was only available on birthdays and shuddered at the thought.

There was silence. What had seemed an open and shut case just four days ago was rapidly unravelling before their eyes. He looked around the room at the blank faces.

"Look, is there anyone in this room who still thinks he did it?" Tom directed the question at all of them. All responded with a shake of the head.

"It's our job to prove he killed Sally. It isn't good enough to present no more than a hunch or a best guess, if anyone disagrees, leave the room now," Tom was serious as he looked at each of them. "The lawyer's job is simply to discredit our case, the onus is not on them to prove he didn't do it, simply to cast doubt in our evidence and so far Beadle has done a cracking job of this. So what do we have to go on?"

Tom tore the top sheet off the clipboard with a violent jerk showing he meant business. He held the marker, poised, waiting for someone to talk.

"The murder weapon," as she spoke, Abi emphasised the word 'murder', there was no doubt in her mind.

"A set of prints on the plastic covering and the same print on the underside of the filing cabinet drawer and a partial print on the golf club that matches," as Chris spoke Tom wrote the word 'prints' on the sheet.

"Dodgy accounts, and," Bob hesitated before he completed the sentence, "and a motive to kill Sally."

Tom turned around, surprised by Bob's confidence.

"Go on."

The room turned to look at Bob.

"So, I'm Sally. I'm my husband's bookkeeper. The business is doing fine and, as far as I can see, it's all above board. I have seen the receipts and these all tally, I file the paperwork and enjoy the lifestyle that the successful company is giving me."

The team look on attentively as Tom speaks, even Tom who was used to Bob's tales was willing to give him the benefit of the doubt.

"And one day, let's call that day Saturday, I am going through the books and something yells out at me. It's nothing obvious, I am used to £20k deliveries and, like everyone assembled here today, I can be forgiven for thinking that this type of delivery didn't mean anything to me. No, I see something else - something small but significant. I do some more checks and cross referencing to see if there is a pattern. It's not right, in fact, it is so not right that it is blatantly wrong. So I press my husband on this. He sees the whole house of cards come tumbling down. We argue, he panics and he kills me."

Bob looks around the room for some confirmation. He sees blank faces, they don't buy it.

"There was no argument, there was no sign of a struggle. I think something else happens. Gordon panics and calls someone else who is implicated, someone who benefits from the scam that Sally has uncovered," Abi continues the story.

"Sally uncovered the money laundering," Chris chips in.

197

"Money laundering?" Abi asks the question to no one in particular, expecting the universe to provide an answer.

"Yes, of course, money laundering. It's the only way to make sense of these amounts," she continues. "Sally uncovers a money laundering scam. Maybe she doesn't realise the implications of this at first, but she knows it isn't right. She confronts her husband and he contacts the beneficiary of the scam. They return to the house, the accomplice confronts Sally and murders her."

"Wow, that's quite a leap there. But stick with it," Tom says, ripping the sheet off the flip-chart and starts to write on the new sheet.

Money laundering - who benefits and how?

Accomplice with driving gloves - who is he?

"Herein lies the answer to the question of who killed Sally. And I will add one more"

Gordon did NOT kill Sally

"I think Gordon isn't guilty of killing Sally. Boy, he's guilty of a few things - enough to keep him off the golf course for a couple of years, but not murder. And our solicitor friend knows this."

No one disagreed, for the past few days they had been unwittingly proving James Gordon not guilty while simultaneously failing to find the person who was.

Bob picked up his phone and started browsing. "Do any of you have the picture of the sand wedge and Gordon's other clubs to hand?"

"I can get them, what have you got?" Abi quickly dashed out of the office and collected the file from her desk.

He found a picture of the Titelist clubs and compared them to the picture of the clubs found at the house, he showed them to the team.

"I knew that there was something strange with the picture, these are left handed clubs"

Tom picked up the picture and studied it, "Yes. And your point?"

Bob stood up, he was right handed and so he mimics a swing by linking his hands and lifting them over his right shoulder.

"Sally was sat in the chair by the window and was hit just above her left ear. I'm right handed and this feels like a natural swing for me."

He mimicked a swing from the left hand side.

"This doesn't feel so natural, I'm willing to bet that it lacks the power of the swing from the right. I suspect a left handed person would feel the same handicap."

He tried the swing with a single hand and again detected the same limitation when he swung to the left with his right arm.

Tom stood up and tried the same swing.

"Mmm. I'm not sure its conclusive, let's park the idea for now and let me think about that," Tom spoke his concerns, "Right, let's focus. Bob, Chris, you concentrate on the money laundering angle. I want a nice easy to understand report on what you have found by 4 p.m., none of your fancy spreadsheets that you love please, just some basic facts," Chris and Bob nodded.

"Abi, grab yourself a quick sandwich and then let's see what we can find about Gordon's movements on Saturday.

She nodded, stood up with the others and walked out of the room.

❖

Chris had been in the office since 5 a.m. and, aside from a sandwich and enough coffee to keep him awake for a month, he was seriously lacking nutrients. As he walked to the Subway on the Old Stein with Abi he was mentally savouring the foot long sub that was waiting for him.

"So, Jane in Operations is dating this new guy. All is going well and she decides to take him back to her place for a coffee," Abi enhanced the word 'coffee', "in fact, the coffee was looking so appealing that the two of them were almost devouring each other as they got to her front door."

"And she has told you this?" Chris looked confused, he guessed the story was going to be lurid and couldn't believe that such details would be shared.

"Yes, of course. She told me to keep it secret, OK? So don't tell anyone"

Chris shrugged, he doubted that he was the first to hear the tale and to be told to keep it secret.

"So she got the key in the door, they almost fell inside and there's this loud racket, something hammering away. She wasn't sure what it was, but she ran into the kitchen and was listening to the appliances, nothing. She went upstairs to the boiler and listened to it, again nothing."

"Where is this going Abi?"

"Her date had followed her upstairs, you know Eric from Traffic?"

He didn't, but he realised that the detail in the secret story was increasing by the minute.

"Anyhow, Eric says the noise is coming from her bedroom. And she says to him, 'Oh, you're in a rush. Anyhow, there's nothing in there. I think it's the attic. If I get a chair, can you go up in the attic and check for me?', and he agrees. She pops downstairs to get a chair."

"And Eric lets himself into the bedroom, I assume?"

'Yep, he opens the door. Her clothes are all over the floor, she had planned to tidy quickly while he drank his coffee. He walks in and can hear the noise getting louder. He looks around the bedroom and can't see anything, but the noise is coming from somewhere. He moves to the side of the room and suspects the noise is coming from the corner, under the clothes. So he lifts the clothes."

Abi starts laughing uncontrollably.

"Ok, he lifts the clothes. And then what?" Chris can tell from Abi's tears that this is going to be funny.

"So, he lifts the clothes and he finds the cause of the noise."

"And?"

"Well it's not her electric toothbrush."

"No! How embarrassing!"

"It gets worse. The 'not electric toothbrush' is turned on and was touching the radiator in the room, hence the noise through the house. He lifts it up and the loud noise stops, but it is still turned on and

201

vibrating. So he's got this dildo in his hand and trying to work out how to turn it off when in walks Jane."

"No! I bet he felt like dying on the spot?"

"He did. Are you not worried about Jane? She was mortified."

Both were laughing with tears coming down their face.

"What can I get you?" The Subway worker was asking them for their order.

"The foot long vegan special please."

The two looked at each other and considered the order and fell about laughing even more.

Abi and Chris were still laughing when they got back to the office.

"Something has obviously tickled you kids, care to explain?" Tom called out.

They looked at each other before both answering.

"Just a private joke," they smiled as they headed to their own tasks.

Tom wandered over to Abi's desk.

"Let's work on the assumption that Gordon has provided incorrect information about his movements on Saturday, this will be in line with everything else he has told us already. The two people he said he was with have vaporised as well."

Abi looked at her notes, "So we can discount the Black Lion?"

"Yup. I don't think that is where he went and it will take hours to trawl through videos and find out he wasn't there. Let's go with what we do know - ANPR."

ANPR, or Automatic Number Plate Recognition, is the system that uses optical character recognition to detect number plates as they pass surveillance cameras. A short drive along the Brighton seafront will result in a single car's numberplate being tracked around half a dozen times. Other cameras around the city will keep a close eye on other streets. With the correct paperwork the police can track a car journey on a turn-by-turn basis.

"Didn't we do that when we picked him up?"

Tom chose not to answer her, he looked at her and waited for her to work this out herself. She slapped her forehead with an open hand.

"Of course! We tried to trace Gordon's car, but he was driving Sally's. He gave us the wrong number, accidental or intentional, who knows?"

"We'll make a detective out of you yet," Tom smiled as he spoke, "Put the request in, it will take a few hours, and work on the carparks whilst you are waiting. Unless he parked on the street, the carpark will have picked up his plate."

Abi turned to her computer unlocked the screen and started her search straight away.

Aside from regular trips to the coffee machine, the team remained buried in their computer terminals, with Bob and Chris adding data to an ever increasing spreadsheet and Abi plotting the movements of

James Gordon. At 4 p.m. Tom called them into the meeting room.

"Who wants to go first?" Tom looked around the room for takers, Abi took the initiative.

"I have plotted the route on a map with times, and a quick summary. First of all, everything is based on Sally's car. We are assuming that Charles was driving, but we have no confirmation of this. All that we know for certain is that his car was at Cooksbridge station all day Saturday.   This could be Sally driving, but let's work on the assumption it wasn't."

Tom nodded his approval.

The first sighting was at 10.45, Sally's car came down Ditchling Road; cameras clocked him three times in total. He carries on down Grand Parade and onto the Old Steine to the seafront, turns right at the pier and then disappears. The next camera is at the junction with West Street, so I assume he turned off into one of the car parks before then. There is parking at the Jury's Inn and the Old Ship, but let's assume he parked in the Lanes car park. I have a request with all three for details."

"That's good, it also ties in with his statement that he went to the Black Lion?" Bob asked the question more of a prompt, silently saying 'keep going'.

"Yes, it could be the Black Lion, but let's work on the assumption it isn't. There must be a couple of dozen choices within five minutes of there. I can ring around, but it will take a few days to go through security footage to find out which."

"Credit or Debit cards?"

"I have checked both, no transactions from his known accounts that day. So he goes quiet for a couple of hours when he is clocked again at 13.35 by the Palace Pier roundabout and driving back pretty much the way he came."

"He paid cash, I recall him saying that," Chris flicks through his notes rapidly, "I guess that I was in the pub until around 2 p.m., I didn't think to check. I went and did a bit of shopping, just bits and bobs, and then left around 3 p.m. and drove home. That's what the statement says, unless he went back into Brighton, and we didn't clock him, he's lying."

"Which puts him home around 2 p.m., a full hour before," Abi confirmed.

"Do we have any tracking on his phone," Tom looked to Bob for confirmation.

"Nope. It wasn't turned on. A couple of years ago it would be on by default, but these days you have to enable. We can request that his phone be triangulated and to raise the paperwork with the phone company."

Tom nodded.

"OK, good work, Abi. Let's try and disprove more of the timing of his statement, but it would also be nice to find something that corroborates it in some way. Anything!" Tom's eyes pleaded as he spoke.

There was a short silence, Abi was finished, so it was time for Chris to chip in. He passed copies of his spreadsheet to Tom and Abi, Bob already had a copy.

"What's this? I asked for a summary and you give me a telephone directory."

"Do they still do telephone directories?" Chris acknowledged the joke and replied with his own. "Sorry it's so bulky, but as they say, data is nothing without context. I am stuck for context, but something is yelling 'laundering' at me."

Tom looked at Bob, who nodded his confirmation.

"OK, take us through what you've got."

For another 15 minutes. Chris took the team through the data he had assembled. He had drawn the money laundering conclusion but lacked the key to unlock it. The meeting was brought to a close and the team wandered back to their desks to clean up for the evening.

"Got your date," Abi's personal phone had buzzed during the meeting and the unanswered text message was creating an itch as the phone remained in her pocket. It was unprofessional to check it in the meeting, but it was the first thing that took her attention as they left the room.

"What?"

"A date, with Carl."

"Carl?"

"He's Bumble's friend, remember? You were interested, so I said yes on your behalf. Tomorrow evening."

"What the fuck?" Chris looked exasperated.

"Hey, it's a double date. Bumble and I will play chaperone to make sure he keeps his dick in his pants. What's the worry?"

"What's the worry? Can't I schedule my own private life? I didn't even know his name until now."

"And now you do. Look, if I left it to you, it would be weeks before you'd even text him. This way you can meet him in a safe environment and if I approve, you can book a second date."

"If you approve? Do I get a say in this?"

"Not, for now. I have texted and said yes, so bring a change of gear and we will leave straight from work tomorrow."

Chapter Nine

Chris arrived just before 8 a.m. and Abi was already sat at her desk.

"Looking good, going on a date tonight?"

He looked down at his clothes; he didn't feel he looked any different from the day before. In fact, he was wearing the same jacket and trousers and he had only changed the shirt. The greeting from Abi had caused a few others in the office to turn around and look at him.

"Leave it out, Abi. It's only a drink with friends. Actually a drink with two people I don't know and one serious pain in the arse."

She turned to a colleague who was grinning at Chris's reaction and said, "I reckon he's keen."

The colleague nodded and blew a kiss at Chris.

He quickly tried to change the subject, "Who's the boss with?"

Abi turned her head to the office, where Tom was in deep discussion with a lady dressed in a smart suit.

"Not sure, they were in there when I arrived."

"Beryl Granger," the colleague who had blown Chris a kiss confirmed, "She is from the CPS, she grabs the big cases"

"Is that good or bad?"

The colleague shrugged a non-committal response and went back to their work.

Chris sat down and logged into his computer. Pulling up the

spreadsheet and staring at the details, he was unsure what he was looking at.

Just under an hour later, the office door opened and Beryl left, shaking Tom's hand. He looked over at the team and signalled for them to come over, they locked their computers and wandered in.

"That was Beryl Granger from the CPS, she handles the murder cases in Sussex. Her office was contacted by Charles Beadle yesterday and she has a meeting with him shortly."

"Is that unusual?" Abi asked.

"Not really, it's the job of every lawyer to look out for their client and it makes sense, given the noise over the last few days, that he would try and press the case early. I have just gone through the case with her, so she is forearmed."

"And?" Abi prompted Tom for more detail.

"And? And we will have to see. I was honest with her, so if we don't find something to warrant keeping James inside much longer, we will have to let him go."

The mood dropped immediately. None of them thought he was responsible, or at least solely responsible, for Sally's death, but felt that if he were freed this would be game over.

"So we have to double our efforts today. How's the spreadsheet going, Chris?"

"Slowly, I can't see the context yet."

"OK, park this for a while. I want you to grab a couple of footballs and a golf club and try your swing. Bob may have a point, I'm not sure, but let me know how it feels. You're not a golf player, so you haven't developed a swing yet. Let's try some raw data."

Chris looked bemused, but acknowledged the request.

"Abi, I am instructing you to go to the pub today. Cast an arc between West Street, North Street and the pier, take a photo of James Gordon with you and ask if he came in on Saturday," Tom couldn't help smiling as he requested this of Abi.

"Do you realise just how many pubs are in that small area?"

"Quite a few and hopefully by the end of the day you will be able to tell me. Don't stay too long, keep it down to just one drink in each."

Abi smiled, she knew that it would be a dry day but appreciated the humour.

"And Bob, can you draft up what we have to date? What we know and what we don't know. What was it that Donald Rumsfeld said?"

'You want the known knowns, the known unknowns, and the unknown unknowns," Bob chose to paraphrase the quote.

"Yep, that's what I need. That's what Beryl will need as well. Fingers crossed that all goes well with the magistrate today."

Working on the assumption that Gordon had parked his car in the Lane's car park, Abi decided to start there. She parked up, locked the doors and walked up the stairs to the surface, glancing at the parking costs as she did.

"£3.50 an hour? Daylight robbery," she muttered to herself, making a mental note to collect a receipt on the way out, there was no way she was subsidising the taxpayer on this one.

Where to start? She looked at Google maps and studied the problem that awaited her. She could already count 20+ pubs, bars and wine bars and that didn't include the various other places that sold alcohol, such as cafes.

Start with the unexpected, a message that had stayed with her through the months of detective training. She had already decided that he hadn't gone to the Black Lion, but thought it sensible to start there all the same.

"Detective Thomson," Abi held up her warrant card as she introduced herself, "do you have a couple of minutes?" She signalled to a seat by the window.

"Sure, 2 secs."

Abi moved to the seat and watched as the bar lady whispered to a colleague before joining her.

"How can I help you, detective, erm?"

"Thomson, but call me Abi."

"OK, how can I help you Abi? I'm Reg."

"Reg?"

"Long story, how can I help?"

Abi scrolled through her pictures on the phone and found a picture of James Gordon, she held the display towards Reg.

"James Gordon?"

"Yes, do you know him?" Abi seemed surprised by the immediate reaction. Maybe she was wrong about the Black Lion.

"His picture is all over the Argus," she reached behind Abi and extracted a copy of the Argus from the window sill. "Same picture, if I'm not wrong?"

"Ah. Of course," It wasn't the same picture but was very similar, a formally dressed James Gordon, "Well, yes, I'm trying to track his movements last Saturday between 11 a.m. and 2 p.m. Do you know if he came in here during this time?"

"Steve," Reg yelled at her colleague behind the bar, motioning her head for him to join them. He walked over.

"Steve, you were working on Saturday. Did you see James Gordon come into the bar on Saturday?" The mention of Gordon's name and no reference to the photo on her phone confirmed how infamous Gordon had become.

"Not that I recall. I was here from opening through to 8 p.m. It's quiet until around midday and then gets busier, but I don't remember seeing him. Of course, someone else may have seen him, but they aren't on shift today."

The scale of her search was just starting to register. Abi reached into her pocket and took out her business card with her contact details.

"Can you ask them? Maybe give them a call? If they did see them, is there any chance you could get them to call me?"

"Of course," Reg and Steve answered in unison.

"Thanks," she stood up and walked out, pondering her next move.

The Cricketers reported the same, no sight of Gordon.

She turned right and walked towards the seafront.

Her next stop was the Hotel de Vin, a wine and cocktail bar. She had ventured into this bar a few times on club nights, sipping the expensive cocktails but not getting the same excitement that her friends had experienced. She got the same answer, they recognised the picture immediately but had no recollection of Gordon visiting on Saturday.

She went to the bar in the Ship Hotel, same response.

The phone rang once and Chris answered.

"Pissed already?"

"A record for me, four bars and not tasted a drop. Chris, can you do me a favour?"

"Sure, fire away."

"Do you have any photos of Gordon that don't look like the one in the Argus?" After she had left the Ship hotel, she realised that the formal image from the Argus was prejudicing people before they even started. Was he the type of guy who would go to the pub on a Saturday in a suit and tie?

Chris knew instinctively what Abi was asking and opened up the picture file on his computer, muttering to himself as he scrolled through the images. When the information had been downloaded from the iCloud that had allowed them access to the business documents, there was also a large library of photos from Sally's phone. Chris scrolled through the images, selected three and forwarded them to her.

"Take a look at these."

She looked at the email and the images attached.

"Perfect, thanks."

"No problem, I will find a few more and send them," as Chris spoke she dropped the call.

The next stop was the Mesmerist. She held up the photo, this time it was a more casual shot of him in jeans and t-shirt, his demeanour was more relaxed than formal. The barman didn't recognise the image as Gordon and, as a result, looked a little closer. He showed it to his colleagues and they also studied and nodded their non-recognition.

She left the pub slightly more enthused, a long afternoon ahead.

The first challenge was to find a golf club. He walked the floor, asking if anyone had any clubs with them. He assumed, correctly, that a few of them were golfers and maybe they had packed a set in the car with the intention of having a game after work. Initially, no one was able to help, until someone suggested the receptionist.

"Try Harry on the front desk. He's the only one with a guaranteed home time and he's a keen *player*." They emphasised the word '*player*' mockingly.

Chris walked to the reception to find Harry, a middle-aged man with a comb over haircut and drab suit that yelled 'single' but was highly deceptive as the rumour mill in the office made clear he was having a second wave of dating courtesy of Tinder.

"Harry, the guys tell me you like a game of golf?"

"Whenever I can, how can I help?"

"Don't suppose you have your clubs on you, do you?"

"Of course, two sets. Male or female?"

"Is there a difference?" Chris admitted his total ignorance of the game.

"Large or medium?" He looked Chris up and down, "Let's say large. I assume you want to borrow some for a game? A date maybe?" He smiled as he spoke, as a recent convert to Tinder, he was bemused why anyone was in a permanent relationship these days.

"Official work. I will only need them for an hour or so."

"Watch the desk for two minutes, I'll be right back."

He walked away from the desk, before turning around and yelling, "Don't try and help anyone; just keep them there. I'll be back soon."

The sudden departure of Harry had shocked Chris, he had no idea what to do if anyone came to reception so he was relieved when told to just keep them there. Before anyone came to the desk, Harry was back.

"One of the benefits of working on reception, my own marked bay right by the stairs. Well, I mark it with a few cones each evening as I leave," he winked.

Chris knew straight away which bay he was talking about, the cones were a permanent fixture and everyone assumed it wasn't available.

How cheeky, he thought.

He lifted the clubs and handed them to Chris.

"They're not expensive, but they're mine. So look after them, please."

Chris studied the set and went straight to the one that looked like a sand wedge.

"Need a bit of practice in the bunkers," he winked at Harry as he walked back into the office, using the club as an exaggerated walking stick.

The ceiling in the office didn't appear to be that low, but as he lifted the club to swing it he realised that a few tiles would be knocked out of place if he persisted for too long. Like many old offices, it was common that the ceilings had been lowered or the floors raised to accommodate space for computer cabling and extra power sockets. A quick trip to the next floor confirmed the same, so he headed to the underground car park which, thankfully, offered more head room.

He started by trying to swing the club sideways, first with his right hand and then with his left hand, trying to get a feel for the swing; both felt the same. He leaned the club against the wall and rushed upstairs to grab an office chair and a chocolate tin.

Tom had suggested a football but he didn't want to trek around the office in search of a ball, so he picked up the chocolate tin that had been there for weeks, left by a colleague - an offering for their birthday. He opened the tin and saw a few chocolates remained, orange creams always seemed to be the least favourite. He tipped these out, placed the empty tin on the chair and wheeled out of the building, down the ramp and into the car park. The chair just fitted below the barrier, which he ducked under.

He lifted the chair to its full height and lifted the headrest as high as it would go. He pictured Sally's head in the chair slightly below the headrest, so he dropped the height a few inches and sat the open end of the tin on the head rest.

He walked away from the chair and studied the reconstruction. He walked forward at speed and swung the club with his right hand, hitting the tin square and kicking it off its perch. He tried a few more times, each time the tin rattled along the garage floor.

He tried the club in his left hand, it felt awkward. He swung and missed. He tried again, the closest he got was just clipping the tin. This wasn't his normal hand, explaining his lack of success.

Chris put the club back in his right, but this time swung across his body, trying to strike the tin from the left hand side. Each time he connected, but the force wasn't enough to knock off the tin. He moved the seat and tin in front of Harry's car and rushed up the stairs and into the office.

"Anyone here cack handed?" Chris called across the office.

"Anyone here prejudiced against non-right handers?" A colleague answered him, "I assume you mean a leftie?"

No time for political correctness, Chris thought of the number of times his sexuality had been referred to 'in jest'.

"Give me 5 minutes of your time, Mr. Cack Leftie," he motioned for him to join him. The colleague noticed the excitement in his voice and followed him without question.

"Right, what I want you to do is swing the club at the tin as hard as you can." The tin was starting to look battered and there was no way that the lid, which still sat forlornly on the seat of the chair, would ever fit again.

The colleague held the club in his left hand and swung from the left.

"Like this?"

"Yes, give it all you can."

He swung the club and connected with the tin, sending it rattling along the concrete floor. Chris picked the tin up and replaced it on the headrest.

"And again."

After another half dozen attempts, he had hit every time and knocked off the tin each time, bar one.

"Ok, now try swinging across your body, and hitting on the righthand side," Chris motioned as he spoke.

The colleague tried again, having the same lack of success as Chris did with the alternative swing.

The initial hearing in the Magistrate's Court is a formality, the prosecution presents the charges, the defendant confirms their name and address, pleads not guilty; and is then remanded in custody. Despite the presence of lawyers, a defendant dressed in their Sunday best, and the drama of the occasion, the whole affair is invariably dull and a foregone conclusion.

This time, though, the authorities feared a different result and the presence of Beryl Granger, instead of an underling, was needed to give Tom the confidence things would go smoothly.

James Gordon had left the detention suite in the Group 4 van, clear in the knowledge that he would not be returning. He would either be bailed or remanded in prison, his confidence was in contrast to that of Tom. As he sat in the van, a bright bulb compensating for the lack of light offered by the darkened windows, he tried to picture the journey from Hollingbury to the court in Edward Street as he was shifted when the van turned. He was driven to the underground car park and escorted to a small, nondescript cell to await his turn in court. He was oblivious to the hoards of reporters who had assembled outside the building, balloting each other for the limited seats to report from inside the small court.

Tom walked into the court with Beryl and they took their seats, both acknowledging Charles Beadle who was awaiting the arrival of James.

The magistrates walked in, took their place and signalled to an assistant, who opened the door and led James in.

James had visited a magistrate's court twice in his life, both times for speeding offences. Each time he sat outside the courtroom with others waiting to be called. He had entered the main door and was directed to sit down, no one gave him a second glance. Five minutes later, he left the room with a fine and three points on his license.

This time around, as he entered the court, via a staircase from the basement where his cell was located, all eyes were on him and journalists were jotting notes, describing his appearance and demeanour in their note books as they tried to take it all in.

Tom started to feel the strain, Beryl looked towards him and mouthed, "OK."

Five minutes later, it was all over. As expected, James Gordon had confirmed his name and address, he didn't make a plea. Unexpectedly, his solicitor made no request for bail. James was to be remanded to prison and appear before a Crown Court at a later date. Before he was led from the courtroom, through the door he entered, the journalists sprung up, as if in unison, and dashed outside to the waiting cameras to report.

Tom and Beryl stood up and walked towards the station, ignoring requests for a statement from the waiting journalists. Five minutes later, they were ensconced in the same meeting room that Abi and Chris had seen them in a few hours before.

"What the fuck was all that about?" Tom asked the question, but the same words were on Beryl's mind.

"He sure likes to play games, doesn't he?"

"Doesn't he just? Maybe he has another surprise waiting for us?" Tom mouthed the words, but his mind was elsewhere. Beryl noticed his change of demeanour.

"What's on your mind?"

"Not sure, but I think I now know who is feeding the Argus."

"Beadle! Of course," Beryl acknowledged Tom.

"Can we catch up later? I need to talk this through with the team.

Meet, say 6 p.m?"

"Ok," Beryl said, standing up to leave the office.

"Actually, can I ask another question? Beadle, have you ever seen him before?"

Beryl thought for a while before answering, "Now you come to mention it, no."

"Is that unusual?"

"You mean, do I know all of the local solicitors? Of course not, but it is pretty unusual to see someone so experienced whom I have never met"

Tom followed her out, stopped at the doorway and gestured to Bob to join him.

By 3 p.m. Abi had entered over 20 pubs, bars and cafes in the area and asked the same sets of questions. She had shown the informal photograph and was met by shakes of the head, she then identified James Gordon and saw the immediate recognition. No one had seen him on Saturday but agreed to ask the other staff when they arrived, each taking a business card from her.

The Druid's Head is a large cavernous bar at the edge of the Laines. On busy nights, the place would be crammed, all seats taken and the remaining space occupied by punters standing and shouting at each other as they tried to combat the noise. On a Thursday afternoon, the lunchtime crowd had left and it would be a couple of hours before the crowds returned in the evening. Two bar staff were present, one was scrolling through stories on his mobile phone and the other responded to Abi's presence. She showed the picture again, identified it as James Gordon and registered another negative response.

"I don't suppose you're still serving food, are you?" Abi was starting to feel hungry, it would be another four or so hours before she would eat.

"Not really, but I can ask the kitchen staff if they have anything? Can I get you a drink while you're waiting?"

Abi stared at the beer pumps and was sorely tempted, but she was on duty.

"A pint of blackcurrant juice and lemonade, please."

She took the drink and went to sit down, checking the map for the remaining locations. As she sipped the drink, the barman came over bearing a plate of chips.

"I'm afraid it's take it or leave it," he smiled.

"I'll take it. Thanks," She reached into her pocket to get some change.

"They're on the house. Another 30 seconds and they would be in the bin."

"Thank you," Abi acknowledged him and started to pick up the chips with her fingers while browsing the map on her phone.

"You're a copper. I can tell coppers a mile away," the stranger had been sitting a few tables away, one of only three other customers in the bar.

"Guilty," Abi smiled, trying to humour him.

"I knew it. I can always tell a copper. Something about your presence," he said, moving closer breathing his alcohol fumes in her direction. The chips started to taste unpleasant.

"How can I help you?"

"You see, it's a talent I had to learn. It would have helped me when I was younger, but sadly, it took a couple of visits inside for me to realise how important a skill this would be," he laughed out loud as he spoke.

"But, get this, as soon as I become a straight and legal citizen, I develop the skill. What use is it to me now?"

"I'm very pleased to know that you're straight and legal now, you seem such a nice guy and I would hate to have to talk to you officially," Abi tried to be pleasant but realised her mistake as he pulled up a chair as if she had welcomed him

Abi stuffed a few more chips into her mouth and drained the remaining drink in a few gulps. She stood up.

"Well, it was a pleasure to meet you. I'm so happy that we won't have to meet on an official basis. But I have to leave now," time to go she thought. A police officer's life is not a happy one, as the saying goes.

"Are you investigating the James Gordon case?"

She was tempted to just acknowledge him and leave. Another ghoul keen for lurid details yet to make the newspapers. But her gut was telling her something else.

"Yes, do you know Mr Gordon?"

"No, I don't know him, but I can tell you where he was on Saturday."

Abi sat down.

"You see, the mistake is to ask the publicans. They're always busy working and not likely to recognise anyone. What you need is a punter who spends his days in the bar."

"And I guess you're one of these punters?" As she asked the question, she knew the answer. Every pub seemed to have the permanent guest who sat in the corner sipping their beer all day, willing to offer their opinion on world matters to anyone who dared to strike up a conversation with them. Judging by the smell of beer on his breath and his general demeanour, he looked just like that guy.

"He was here on Saturday," the stranger pointed to a table in the corner, "he was sitting over there. He managed to down a few pints in a short space of time and was arguing with the other guy. I saw his picture in the paper and recognised him."

Abi sat upright, a lead at last.

"And the other guy?"

"Similar type."

"Similar type?"

"You know, the type of guy who wears a suit all week but still looks the part in jeans and a casual shirt at the weekend," the stranger gestured to himself, "I'm the other type. I couldn't brush up if I tried."

"Could you come a make a statement in the station?"

"And only two minutes ago you were telling me you didn't want to see me on an official basis," he laughed loudly.

Abi called the station and asked for a car to collect them.

Considering he spent his waking hours sitting in the pub drinking, the stranger presented himself clearly and coherently, a functioning alcoholic would be an apt description.

His name was Simon Windsor. As a young man he was in and out of trouble with the law and, as Abi had checked afterwards, had been a guest of her Majesty on two occasions. In his mid twenties, he had gone straight and set up a successful business, importing goods and supplying local traders. All went well until his wife decided to call it a day and left, taking her share. He borrowed the money to buy her out and, thanks to crippling interest rates and his lack of focus, the company folded a couple of years later. He had spent the past three years sitting in local bars, drinking away the hours. She was expecting a life story and he was more than willing to provide one.

"Let's chat for now and then we can draft a statement together, if that's OK?"

"Works for me."

"So what time were you in the Druids Head and what time did you see Gordon arrive?"

"I usually arrive just after 11a.m., I'm a bit of a creature of habit these days. I sit in my usual spot, reading a book or a paper, while trying to keep the beer count to single figures and then leave around 5 p.m."

"And this is your daily routine?" Abi tried to imagine how successful he was at keeping the count to single figures as the beer fumes filled the small interviewing room they were sitting in.

"Pretty much. Anyhow, I started to notice them around 12."

"Started to notice them?"

"Yes, I didn't see them come in as it's a busy time around Saturday lunch, but they were getting gradually louder, I couldn't help but notice them."

"Did you hear what they were saying?"

"No, too many punters and a few tables between us. But the discussion did get louder and he became agitated. The other guy remained calm throughout. I'm not sure what they were talking about.

"Agitated? In what way?"

Simon stood up, walked around the table. Sat down, held his head in his hands, stood up and sat down again.

"Like that. He couldn't sit still, he clearly had something on his mind and the other guy wasn't helping," Windsor's animated description of agitation was quite clear.

"Can you describe the other guy?"

"Not really, he had his back to me, whereas Gordon was facing me.

He was dressed smart, but casual."

"And they left together? What time?"

"Yes, they left together. Walked to the door and then I forgot about them, until I saw the report in the Argus. Time wise, probably just after 1 p.m., I was just ordering my 4th pint."

Four pints by 1 p.m.? He would seriously struggle to keep the count to single figures at that rate, Abi thought.

She had been taking notes and working out how to prepare the statement to capture the information. She picked up a pad of numbered A4 sheets and looked to Simon.

"OK, let's try and change what you have said into a statement. We can discuss the sentences and, if you agree with the wording, I will write it down and you can sign the statement. Is that OK with you?"

"Sure, let's go for it."

Bob called the team into the office, he looked at his watch. He was expecting Beryl Grainger at 6 p.m, he had 45 minutes spare.

Abi started with a summary of her meeting with Simon Windsor, describing the habitual pub goer who grabbed his first beer every morning at 11 a.m. and drank through to 5 p.m. before heading home. The team acknowledged, most bars in Brighton have their own resident drinkers and Windsor was the Druids'.

"He has provided a clear statement," as Abi spoke, she handed out copies of the statement to the others, who read as she quickly summarised.

"He has described James arguing with another person, with no details other than casually dressed but smart with it. James was described as agitated and the other person calm," Abi stood up and walked around the offices using Windsor's action to mimic the agitation. She sat back down.

"He is unsure of what time they arrived, but is confident that Gordon and the other person left around 1 p.m."

"Which ties in with the timeline," Chris commented as he checked his notes.

"Is he a reliable witness? He seems to spend a lot of the time in the pub and most of that drinking," Tom spoke, had been caught out before with fantasists looking for their moment in the limelight.

"I would call him a functioning alcoholic. To be honest, if I hadn't met him in a pub and smelled the beer on his breath, I would be none the wiser as to his sobriety."

"Or lack of it," Chris joked.

"Indeed, or lack of it. He is a recently failed businessman. He did his time years ago. Yes, I think he's reliable." Abi spoke of her confidence in the witness.

"And we know where to find him if we need to talk to him again, by all accounts?" Chris smiled as he spoke.

"So if you want my address, it's number one at the end of the bar," Bob sung the words as he spoke. Chris and Abi looked confused.

"Marillion."

"Who?" They spoke in unison.

"Marillion. You guys have never heard of Marillion? You have never lived," Bob said as he looked to an equally bemused Tom for some encouragement.

"Ok Chris, maybe you can tell us something that will cause Bob to break into song as well?" Tom spoke as he turned to Chris.

"Are we sure James Gordon is left handed?" Chris started with a question.

The team shrugged.

"Nope, I didn't notice either," he spoke, going on to explain his theory and how the blow had to come from someone who was right handed, given the position of Sally and her wound.

"If he is left-handed then I don't believe he struck Sally. We need to check," Chris was adamant in his findings, but this was meaningless until they knew.

"Give me ten minutes, I can get you the answer," Bob jumped up and left the office.

Chris elaborated on his theory and spoke of how the swing was lacking if it was backhanded. As Bob re-entered the office, the three of them were stood up, swinging a pretend golf club with different hands.

"He's a lefty." Bob confirmed.

"Really, how can you be sure?"

"My friend works at Lewes, the receptionist transferred me to him, and, as luck would have it, he's on the same wing. Got him to ask James to sign something and he confirmed?"

"Sign something? What did he sign?"

Bob shrugged, "Who knows. It's his first day inside and he would sign away his mum because he is so confused. But he definitely signed with his left hand."

Tom looked outside of the office, he could see Beryl Grainger walking towards them.

"Ok, let's resume first thing. I suspect that Mr. Gordon will be heading home by the weekend."

Tom gestured to Beryl and the others left.

❖

Chris and Abi wandered back to their desks and Chris made a move to logon to the computer.

"No you don't," Abi spoke the words with an authority that made Chris freeze, he turned towards her with his fingers still poised over the keyboard.

"No I don't what?"

"No, you don't login, its almost 6 p.m. and we will be heading to the pub shortly. I know you, you'll login and I will have to prise you away from the keyboard. Grab your stuff, have a quick shower, and meet me in reception at 6.30"

"A shower? I wasn't planning to have a shower."

She laughed, leaning towards him and exaggerating a sniff. "Some date you'll make, the same clothes all day smelling like that. Go grab a shower, I'll see you in reception after I've had mine."

Abi spoke with the same authority that prevented him from logging onto his PC. He reached in his drawer and took out the toothbrush and toothpaste. There would be towels in the changing rooms and someone would have left some shower gel.

Fifteen minutes later, after rushing a shower, towelling off and dressing, he walked to the reception, shocked to see Abi in a fresh set of clothes and her hair neatly brushed. He couldn't imagine how anyone could have gotten themselves ready so quickly.

"Right, let's go. They should be there by 7 p.m. so you can grab some Dutch courage before they arrive. She walked towards the door to the car park and suddenly froze.

"Fuck!"

"What's up?"

"Fuck, fuck, fuck!"

"Are you going to give me a clue Abi?" Chris looked confused as he spoke.

"My car is in the fucking Lane's carpark. I took a police car back here with Windsor and forgot that my car was still parked there. It's £3.50 an hour, daylight fucking robbery. We'll have to get a taxi there and collect it."

She looked at Chris who was smirking, he knew better than to offer advice at this stage.

"And none of your advice," Abi confirmed Chris's thoughts.

He started to offer a suggestion but realised that it was futile as she grimaced even as he started to form the words on his lips.

"OK, schtum then," he exaggerated the response by drawing an imaginary zip over his lips. He remained silent while Abi made the call for a taxi. The car arrived and they continued the drive in silence. Only when the taxi dropped them off did she start to lighten up.

"Can I talk now?" His smile started the sentence, she smiled back. All was good.

"Wait here," she walked into the carpark. Less than five minutes later, she drove up the exit ramp. He got in.

"£21. Do you think the boss will sign this off?"

"Yes," Chris knew the answer was more likely no, but decided to let her save her reaction for later.

The Smuggler's Rest sits on the seafront in Peacehaven, between Brighton and Newhaven. It wasn't the usual choice for either Abi or Chris, but it had one advantage in that it wasn't frequented by their colleagues.

Peacehaven is a small town that was built shortly after WW1 for returning heroes, originally named new-Anzac-on-sea. Abi was the unwilling recipient of this information. When Chris was nervous, he was either dead quiet or, as in this case, chattering at nineteen to the dozen. He was deliberately avoiding the case but equally avoiding talking about his date. He filled the gap by talking about everything else.

"You know, he's not going to be the slightest bit interested in how the Meridian line passes through this place. Nor is he going to be interested in the undercliff walk from Brighton. Just cool it Chris, try and stay calm."

"Am I talking too much," he looked over at Abi who was feigning mock shock. "OK, I'll cool it. What time are they due to arrive?"

"I told them 7.30, it's quarter past now. We can grab a drink and calm down for a short while," Abi spoke as she pulled the car into the carpark and immediately saw Bumble get out of the car with his friend.

"Spoke too soon. There they are," Abi looked over at Chris who had suddenly sprouted a smile. "Well, I don't know about you, Chris, but I certainly would."

Chris opened the door before the car had stopped.

"Cool, Chris. Cool," she reminded him.

He got out of the car and walked towards them. That was the point that he realised he had forgotten his date's name.

"Well, you must be Bumble, and," he hesitated, "you must be .."

"Carl," he walked to Chris and kissed him on both cheeks. "Lovely to meet you."

"And I'm Roger, "Bumble replied. An embarrassing few seconds passed whilst the two tried to establish the correct way of greeting, Roger took the initiative and hugged Chris, who was just about to hold open his hand for a handshake.

Abi leaned forward to hug Roger and kiss him. The two couples walked to the entrance, sharing small talk.

❖

The evening was a blast, Chris took to both Carl and Roger, especially Carl. Abi felt happy that she had managed to introduce them, and she was also happy to spend an evening where they didn't talk shop.

"How about we go and powder our noses and give these two lovers a bit of space?" She looked over at Roger, kicking him so he got the message. They walked to the bar to chat, both glancing over at them.

"Looks like a success to me?" Roger spoke the words that Abi was thinking. "He's a nice bloke, knowing Carl, I think it's a good match."

"I hope so, Chris needs some time away from work. He lives for the job."

Roger signalled to the barman, "Do you have the bill, please?"

"Maybe I will be remembered by them at the wedding as the guy who bought them their first meal?"

"Sweet of you, and thanks," Abi leaned forward and kissed him.

"I'm afraid the card machine is bust. Do you have cash?" The barman repeated the words he had been saying all evening.

Abi and Roger looked at each other, both speaking together.

"Cash?"

"Thought not. Do you have a banking app to transfer the money?"

Roger shrugged, "Sorry."

"Oh well, maybe I will be remembered by them at the wedding as the girl who bought them their first meal? Chris will relish this."

She got out her phone and logged into the application and the bar man passed her the details.

"The account is in my boss's name."

Abi was pleased that she wasn't investigating the tax affairs of the pub, she sighed and started to enter the details.

"It says it's invalid, have I spelled this right, Amie Jarvis?" She looked at the barman. He grabbed the piece of paper from her and passed it to her boss who looked at it and walked towards them.

"Sorry. I forgot, I use my maiden name on this account, please use Cuthbert."

Abi re-entered the name and this time it was accepted, and the money transferred. She showed it to the barman as proof.

"Clever stuff. It checks the bank details and the name?" Roger looked inquisitive.

"Yes, must be a new thing. There was a story back at the station of one of the sergeants who transferred a deposit for a house to the solicitor and got the account number wrong by one digit. It took him weeks to get the money back from the recipient who thought all their Christmases had come at once. He lost the house in the process."

"Poor sod, but a worthwhile change. I bet he wished these changes were in place at the time?"

"Yes, poor sod indeed," as Abi spoke her mind went elsewhere. Roger looked at her but she didn't respond.

"Sorry Roger, something has come up. I going to need to go back to the station," she walked past a confused Roger and towards Chris.

"Chris, I've found the missing piece of the puzzle, I think. We need to go back to the office."

Chris was in a quandary, this was his dream date, but he could also see the look on her face. Carl looked at Chris.

"Don't worry about me, Roger warned me that your job has unusual hours. I would love to see you again. And soon! Text me, please."

"Please don't ever complain to me about being on the job all day, Abi," Chris grinned as he spoke. He clearly understood that it must be important, Abi wouldn't willingly break off a date unless it was important.

Abi stared at the road as she drove in complete silence. She was giving nothing away, this intrigued Chris even more. What was it that caused the sudden rush to the office?

The police station was a 24 hour affair, but as most criminals needed to sleep, just like the good guys, the office was mostly empty. Abi parked the car and climbed the steps into the office, still in silence.

"What is it Abi? What's got you?"

"Do me a favour. Can you transfer £5 to my account?"

Chris started to reply but realised she was serious.

"Open the bank app on your phone," Abi spoke the instructions, "Go to 'Payments and Transfers', that's the one."

Chris followed her instructions.

Chris entered Abi's name and the bank details she gave him and showed the phone to her to check, she nodded. He pressed 'confirm'.

"It says the details are incorrect," Chris passed the phone to her so she could check. She didn't look surprised.

"Change the name to Christine."

"What, Christine? Your name is Christine?"

"Yes."

"So who's Abi?"

"Abigail is my middle name. On day one, when I joined the team, and realised that I would be working with another Chris I decided to change. Imagine Chris Thomson and Chris Thomas? What fun they would have in the office."

"Yes, and our boss Tom Christopher would like it even less." Chris smirked as he spoke. "So you decided to change your name there and then?"

"Yes, an on the spot name change. I was up in HR an hour later to make it official. My family still call me Christine. My mum doesn't even know I use Abi, she would be shocked. Anyhow, change it to Christine and retry."

Chris changed the details and pressed confirm.

"That worked. I'm still smiling at the thought of Chris and Chris."

"Yeah, yeah. This lot don't need any encouragement. Ok, try and send me £5."

He complied. Five seconds later, Abi's phone pinged.

"Woo Hoo! I'm £5 richer. Thanks sucker. Do you have the details of the Allstar account you opened a couple of days ago?" Abi grinned at Chris as she spoke.

"They're on my computer, let me check," Chris logged onto the PC and found the email. The application was accepted almost immediately, he had commented at the time just how ridiculously easy credit was.

"I need the bank details, do you have them?"

The card was still to arrive, but the payment details had come through within the hour.

"Yup, I've got them here."

"OK, time to lose another £5. Pop them in and see what happens."

Again Chris complied, the details went through immediately. He added his account details in the reference field, within seconds his bank account was shy of another £5.

"This is becoming an expensive exercise, Chris, sorry I mean Abi," Chris grinned and Abi grimaced. "I assume you're paid as much as I am?"

"Leave it out, I paid for dinner, OK." She logged into her PC, brought up the documents from the case and scrolled through them until she found the bank statement. "Right, time for you to lose another £5."

"Seriously?"

"Yes seriously, although I don't think we will find this one so easy," Abi said providing the details to Chris.

"Nope, details are wrong. You were expecting this?"

"Kind of, let's try a few changes. Start by changing the name to 'Allstar Enterprises'."

"Same," he started to feel reassured that he would keep his fiver this time.

"Allstar Enterprises Ltd."

"Nope."

She stared at the screen and then the penny dropped. "Try putting a space between 'All' and 'star' and drop the 'Ltd'"

He made the change and started to realise where this was going. He made the change and hit confirm.

"Shit, just lost another fiver," he smiled as he spoke the words. Abi smiled back. "How can someone setup a name of a company with a name used by another company?"

"They can't, but they can setup any name, call it Fred Bloggs Limited and trade as another name."

Chris looked confused.

"My uncle used to work down the road for a company called ABS

Computers," Abi started to explain

"What ABS, as in Anti-lock Braking System?"

"Yes, and as in any number of variations of this acronym. I think you'll find that there are plenty of companies out there trading under ABS. The actual company was called 'Allied Business Systems', but the trading name was ABS. I also recall a company called Van Vliet," Abi pronounced 'Vliet' as Fleet, and spelled the name to illustrate the likely confusion.

"So?"

"Well can you imagine your average guy being asked to make a cheque out to 'Van Vliet'? A few are going to spell it wrong as 'Van Fleet'. What does the accounts department do? Do they return the cheque and ask them to return with the correct name, or do they go to the bank, explain the confusion and ask them to accept it?"

"I assume they do the latter?"

"Exactly. A company can happily trade as any number of names as long as Companies House and the bank are aware. My birth certificate still says Christine and I haven't changed my name by deed poll, I have two accounts in the names of Abi and Christine. All above board."

"So you're saying that All Star Enterprises is a trading name and not related to Allstar - the fuel card company - in any way?"

"Boy! We'll make a detective of you yet."

Establishing that All Star Enterprises was a trading name was the easy part, finding out exactly who the real company was would be a lot harder. As expected, Googling the name didn't help, as Google kept asking, 'do you mean Allstar?'. The only obvious way would be to trace via the bank account, but that required paperwork to be signed off and those who can provide the signatures worked a strict 9-5 shift. It was now 1 a.m. and both were determined to get a head start before then.

They agreed to look at the bank statements and see if they could deduce anything from them.

They started by looking at all the entries for the All Star. These were regular, pretty much the same day each month, allowing for weekends. The amounts differed and were always irregular, none were exact pound amounts. This made sense, companies tended to process monthly payments at the same time each month and no one successfully manages to fill the tanks to an exact amount despite the many attempts to do so.

There was no obvious pattern to the amounts, they seemed totally random. Fuel consumption was not predicable, even when travelling the same journey day in and day out the consumption will be dependent on multiple factors.

Rather than looking at the payments, they looked at the income. Again, this was irregular with no obvious pattern.

Then it struck Abi. "We're looking in the wrong place, let's go through the invoices."

They picked a month at random and totalled them up.

"March, total invoices are £122,451.66, what's the All Star bill for March?"

Chris confirmed, "£24,290.33."

"February, total £145,876,40."

"All Star, £29,175.28."

"June, total £110,450.56. Don't tell me the answer, let me guess," Abi got the calculator application up and made the quick calculation. "£22,090.11?"

Chris was impressed, "Close, £22,090.12. Are you going to tell me your secret?"

"It's 20%. Either the fleet is the most efficient in the country, or this is a total scam. We have always doubted the business model, this is the proof. We need to get all these numbers into a spreadsheet for the boss. You run the invoices and I'll get the All Star costs."

For the next hour they went through the details and produced a spreadsheet of monthly invoices and fuel costs. They added a third column to show 20% of the invoices. For the last three and a half years years the monthly fuel costs were exactly 20% of the invoice amounts, give or take a penny.

"The boss will definitely go for a bank search with these details," Chris looked at his watch. "It's 4.30. What do we do? If I head home now, I will crash and not wake up."

Abi looked to the meeting room, "Maybe we will get a couple of hours here."

Chris agreed, they wandered over to the room, laid down and were asleep within a minute.

Chapter Ten

Chris sensed it first and then Abi a few seconds later. They had been sound asleep, seemingly oblivious to the sounds of colleagues arriving at their desks, but as their sixth sense kicked in and their eyes opened to their boss holding his phone up and taking a picture on the camera.

"That one's going to do the rounds, believe me," he smirked, "Did your mums kick you out or something?"

They looked up and saw the entire office grinning through the glass windows of the office, most with cameras in hand.

Abi turned to Chris. "I guess this is going to be a difficult one to explain?"

"Tell you what," Tom spoke, "You grab yourself a quick shower and some breakfast, it's 8.05, let's meet-up here at 8.45. I hope that you have something exciting to tell me." He could detect the excitement on Abi's face.

"No, leave it for now. If you don't freshen up now, you won't get the chance later."

Forty minutes later, after a quick shower and a breakfast delivered by Uber Eats, they were assembled in the briefing room at 8.45 a.m.

"So what have you guys got?" Asked Tom.

Chris logged onto the computer in the office so he could project the details on to the monitor on the wall. He talked them through the attempts to transfer the money, the payments to All Star Enterprises and the direct coloration of the invoice amounts.

They all smiled when they heard Abi was really called Christine. Tom knew, of course, as he was her incoming boss, but he didn't let on.

Tom was impressed. He lifted himself off the seat and took his wallet from his back pocket, counting out two fivers. He gave them to Chris.

"There you go son, you can get the other £5 back from Abi, I'll argue the expense claim. This is great work. Let's get the paperwork raised to trace this bank account."

Abi nodded and jokingly mouthed, "no way" at the suggestion she refund the other £5.

"Boss," Bob spoke, his head still buried in the documents on his laptop, "I think we need to trace another account."

"Go on."

"Wick Consultants. They only appears every 6 months. The amount is sizeable. Two things come to mind. One, the amounts are 2.5% of the previous six month invoices, give or take a penny. Second, the sort code."

All looked at the details on the screen.

"What's with the sort code?" Abi spoke the words just as she realised, "Ah, it's the same sort code. What are the chances of that?"

"Pretty small, I would guess, unless the account was opened with the same bank branch, and .."

"And by the same person," Chris competed the sentence.

"Exactly, the same branch and the same person. Someone has a nice little scheme going on here."

The paperwork to access the bank account was relatively straightforward, including details of the account and the reason why they required access. The process was not. Abi completed the paperwork, Tom signed it off and then passed it on to the Superintendent who requested more information and an explanation. This had to be clear because it could be questioned another four times as it worked its way through the ranks. The explanation could mutate through this process, but thankfully it stayed the same. Roughly. By 12 p.m. the request had been completed and, suitably armed, they could approach Lloyds Bank for the details. By 1 p.m. it came through.

A parallel, but less urgent, request was also initiated for Wick Consultants. This would come through later, combining the two requests would raise more questions and slow down the process.

Because of GDPR laws, the data provided was minimal, but adequate. A higher level request would be required to gain more detailed information, this would follow. The initial request for bank statements from Brunswick Haulage was more straight forward because it was directly related to a murder investigation. The new request was speculative. For now.

They now had the details of the real company, not just the 'All Star' trading name, a company called Sound Transportation Services Ltd. They also had confirmation of receipt of the payments and names of the account signatories. As expected, three of these names were simply placemen, George Adams, Carl Brown and Sandra Collins - Adams, Brown, Collins - ABC. Some people can't help themselves and make it so obvious, but this made the fourth name stand out.

Kevin Williams.

"He's your guy. Bob, I suggest that you research the other three, but I suspect they will turn up quite a few times. My betting is trainee solicitors who are directors of dozens of companies. Maybe find out who employs them as well, their tax records should show who this is."

Bob stared back at Tom with his 'teach grandma to suck eggs' look.

"Kevin Williams & Sound Transport Services Ltd. Take one a piece and find out what you can about them. Nothing is too trivial at this stage. And be quick. I have Beadle and the CPS breathing down my neck. James Gordon will be a free man tomorrow morning at this rate. Everything we have on him has vaporised. Even I don't think he's done it, I do know one thing: he is key to this. Short of wasting police time I am struggling to find an offence to charge him with."

Without another word, they left the office and started on their tasks.

Referring to his 'teaching Grandma to Suck Eggs' manual, Bob set about tracing the three place men. As expected, he hit pay-dirt within minutes. He googled Sound Transport Services Ltd. and found they had a website of sorts. It was functional, a picture of a lorry driving along a motorway (stock photo he suspected), an 'About' section, some drivel about professional services for haulage companies, and a few other standard drop downs with minimal and noncommittal information.

He Googled independent website designers and took the first hit. They had a mobile number, so he called them. He wasn't surprised when the call was answered in a couple of rings and he found himself talking to the web developer.

"Hello, this is Alf Daniels from JDB Haulage. I am looking for a rough quote on producing a website for my company."

"Of course, I'm your man." Did Bob detect desperation in his voice? "What are you looking for?"

"Well, I'm not a big operation. Just something cheap," he could hear the deflation over the phone, "I have an example website that does what I am looking for; could you take a look?" Bob provided the URL.

He could hear the clicking over the phone and more desperation. He suspected this was the first call the independent web designer had received in a long time and here he was expected to price up the cheapest of jobs.

The clicks continued, maybe in an attempt to make it seem like the job was bigger than expected.

"Should be possible. I could put something together for £3k."

"£3k?" Bob tried to sound confused, IT workers described everything in k.

"£3k, sorry, £3,000."

"Oooh, a bit on the expensive side. Could you do it cheaper?"

If the guy on the end of the phone were a balloon, there wouldn't be much left of him by now, such was the deflation.

"OK, £2k. Payment upfront. I need the order by this evening though, I'm very busy," he lied.

"Sounds good, can you email me the quote and bank details to service@jdbhaulage.business.com?" Bob could hear the balloon inflate, just a little.

"Sure thing, I will get onto it straight away."

Bob hung up. He had made sure that his police phone blocked the number and it would be a couple minutes before the email bounced.

As expected, the Sound Transport Services Ltd. website was a quick mockup. Perfunctory, nothing else. It made a presence but it was doubtful it would attract any business. He clicked on the 'About Sound Transport Services Ltd' section again. There was a link to the directors, every company seemed to have a link to their directors. Bob supposed most have a few narcissistic traits in thinking people were even remotely interested in the backgrounds of the directors. This time, though, Bob was interested.

It showed pictures of all the directors, well, three of them - no surprises there, three pictures of fresh faced adults in smart formal wear and a brief biography of their career, it's amazing how they managed to flesh out less than three years of a career. He was able to find all three on LinkedIn and, no surprise, they all worked for the same company. And, no surprise again, not one mentioned their role as company directors of Sound Transport Services Ltd.

Abi sat at her desk contemplating the best way to investigate Sound Transport Services Ltd. just as Bob rolled over and explained what he had already found out.

"I'll focus on Adams, Brown and Collins. Hopefully this will give you a head start on the company."

Abi was impressed, in the time she had taken to powder her nose, Bob had established that the company website was as vanilla as they come and was designed purely as a means of establishing a presence. She wasn't expecting to find out much about the company.

A quick check on the company via Companies House confirmed the details of the directors and the breakdown of ordinary shares, 100% of which are owned by Williams. It was evident that the legal responsibilities inherited by the other three were not rewarded in any obvious way.

The company was established just over four years ago, around two months before Brunswick Haulage started paying 20% of their income to All Star Enterprises. Every year, a company has to file accounts in arrears. They are allowed a 9 month period after the first year's end to file, so only two years of accounts were available. The accounts didn't break down sales by customer, instead, they were just plain numbers.

They reported just over £210,000 in sales in the first year. Abi checked the spreadsheet and totalled up the first few payments from Brunswick, the first 9 came to £202,000 and the first 10 to £230,000. She suspected that the £210,000 was made up of these first 9 payments and a small amount of 'small jobs' so as to not make the accounts look so obvious.

The second year's sales were £260,000, roughly the same as the next 12 payments plus another £12,000 of sales, just like the previous year.

The company was far from profitable. £180,000 of the first year's sales were listed as outgoings and £240,000 the following year. Quite where this money was going was another question, she needed access to the detailed accounts to find out where, but she suspected it was a single company and, she sighed, another rabbit hole to find out who would be the eventual recipient. She looked again at the filed accounts and saw that these were produced by Pointer Accountancy. She Googled them and found a perfunctory website, not that different from Sound Transport Services Ltd. Only the one partner was listed and a phone number. She picked up the phone and called.

"Pointer Accountancy."

"Hello, my name is Detective Abi Thomas. May I ask who I am talking to?"

"This is Tracy Pointer. How may I help Detective Thomas?"

"Call me Abi," she was keen to drop the formalities as quickly as possible, people are more open to answering questions once they have a first name.

"Yes, how may I help, Abi?"

"I'm calling about a company called Sound Transport Services Ltd. I understand you do their accounts?"

"Yes, how can I help?"

Abi wasn't expecting such a quick and direct answer, she continued.

"That's great, thanks. What can you tell me about them?"

"Not much, to be honest. One of many small companies, they send me their detailed accounts, I audit them and produce signed off accounts that they submit to Companies House. I drop them an invoice and they pay. Repeat the process next year."

"As simple as that? You don't need to visit their offices or anything?"

"Yes, as simple as that. They only raise a dozen or so invoices a year, a few outgoings and expenses. Pretty straightforward. Most of my work is processing these small companies, usually one man bands, freelancers and consultants."

"Do you have their detailed accounts?"

"Yes, of course, My name is on the audit, I'm legally responsible if there is a problem. I can't give you access without the permission of the client or a court order, though," Tracy was quick to pre-empt the next question from Abi. Client confidentiality is a cornerstone of her trade.

"Of course. Please don't contact the client; this is, how can I say, part of an ongoing police investigation."

"I understand. You know the process, so if you get the court order I can help you," Tracy spoke the words but the implied 'without the court order, you're not getting anything' was unspoken.

"OK, just one more question," Abi was flying blind at this point, "you also audit Wick Consultants. I will process both requests on the same order if that is OK?"

"Yes, I audit Wick Consulting and other companies for Mr. Williams. He is one of my major clients."

Bingo!

"Thank you. We will be in touch very shortly," Abi hung up.

She ran to Tom's desk, try as she could there was no way she could casually walk.

"Boss, Williams does run Wick Consultants and, get this, a few other companies. All audited by the same person, Tracy Pointer."

"I suggest that you drive over and bring her in immediately. We don't want her calling Williams so let's get a statement."

She ran back to her desk, walking was no longer an option, and checked the address. Offices on Lewes Road, should be a quick ten minute drive. She grabbed her keys and headed to the car park. Nine minutes later, she pulled into a side street, and two minutes after that she was at the door of the offices.

The buzzer was on the door, she pressed it.

"Hello."

"Hello, Detective Thomas. We spoke a few minutes ago," Abi dropped the informality. This was becoming real.

"Hello Detective Thomas, please come up," there was resignation in her voice, as if she was expecting the visit.

The door clicked and Abi walked up the stairs to the tiny office. A sign on the door read 'Pointer Accounts', Tracy was waiting at the door as she reached the top of the stairs.

"I thought you would be here like a flash. I really can't say anything more until the court order is processed. Client confidentiality, you understand?" Tracy spoke the words as if she were just about to enter a confessional.

"All by the book, Tracy, I promise. Shall we go to the station?"

"Promise you won't look at these files until you have the order?" She looked over at Abi as she spoke, it was more of an instruction than a question. "I should take these with me, can you give me a hand?"

The office was very small and the walls were lined with boxes and boxes of files, Abi suspected that the accountancy practice was not that lucrative, and that the bulk of the files related to Williams. She wasn't too far off.

"I have a suspicion that these won't fit in my Fiat Uno."

Tracy laughed, which was an adequate answer.

Abi called the office and asked for a van to come and collect the files. She waited until they arrived, during which time Tracy had separated the files needed, and left strict instructions with the van driver that the files were to be delivered to the meeting room at the station and not to be opened.

They left in Tracy's car and arrived at the station ten minutes later. As Abi walked Tracy in, Tom looked up, somewhat confused. She signalled Tom to wait.

"Tea or coffee?"

"Coffee, please, black. I think this is going to be a long session," as Abi suspected, a confessional was about to follow.

She left Tracy in the office and walked over to Chris.

"Two coffees, black," Abi was starting to wilt after the all night session, coffee seemed the only answer. Chris looked up with his 'what the fuck' face, Abi responded with her 'just fucking do it' face. Chris got the message.

She walked over to Tom and briefed him quickly.

"I'll sort out the paper work now, just chat generally with her. Get back in there with her now."

As Chris walked in with the coffee, the boxes of files started to arrive and were placed in the office with Abi and Tracy.

Tracy couldn't wait for the court order, and as soon as she got assurances from Abi that the paperwork was in place, she started to talk. And talk.

The crux of it was that the work with Williams was very lucrative. The small office was just a show. The bulk of her work was for Williams, she only took on a few freelancers and contractors, just to flesh out the client list. Williams had paid a premium fee, no questions asked. She had started her accountancy practice in a very simple and standard way, Williams had a small company, generated a single invoice each month and approximately £500 of expenses from various receipted places. All totally above board.

Then he brought in a new company, which generated next to no income, claiming he was developing a consultancy and expected the work to come in soon. Shortly after that, another three companies. Business was blossoming.

"Did you have your Lewes Road office at the time?" Abi wanted to understand how it started.

"No, back then I worked from home. As I said, the bulk of my business was accounting for IT consultants. Brighton attracts a lot of these, a direct one hour journey to London. They raise a monthly invoice of around £10,000 and then submit the odd expenses, mostly for computer equipment." Tracy described her core business model.

Abi considered her pay packet, clearly consultants were being paid a lot more than she was.

"How did they find you? Sorry to be blunt, but your website isn't overly ambitious."

"Google AdSense. Pure and simple, Google 'IT consultancy accountant Brighton' and you'll get a hit."

Abi believed her, the power of the internet never ceased to amaze her, even though, at her age, she couldn't even recall a time before the internet.

"Back to Williams, so where did you meet? Did he come to your house? Or did you meet at his office?"

"His office? Look at the addresses - all modern day equivalents of PO boxes. No, can you believe that I have never met him?"

Abi could, this was starting to sound very much like her man.

"Really? So how did you complete the legal documents? Surely this requires face-to-face meetings?"

"Not at all. I never meet any of my consultants, they register for a limited company online, submit copies of documents via emails. Anything that needs to be signed can be posted, or nowadays people are happy to use DocuSign."

Abi made a note about DocuSign, the name sounded descriptive enough, but she would check to be sure.

"So why the office? It's not exactly luxurious, you had to squeeze past the files to get to your desk."

And so the confessional began.

"I never actually met Mr. Williams. We spoke regularly on the phone, but never face-to-face. I would meet the accountants of his clients now and again, but I didn't think the kitchen table at home, at the time it was my mum's place, was conducive for business. So I told him, and he found this place and paid the rent five years up front."

"Seriously? OK, it's not the most salubrious of places, but 5 years' rent on anything in Brighton doesn't come cheap."

Tracy looked embarrassed as she answered.

"There are many things about the arrangement I have with Mr. Williams that I am not happy with, but once you start, well, you know?"

Abi started to realise the seriousness of this conversation. As much as she would like it to continue, she had to respect Tracy's rights.

"Tracy, you're starting to reveal a lot of information that could incriminate you. You do realise? Maybe you should talk to a solicitor before we go on?"

She took a deep breath to help stem the tears that were starting to form.

"No. I understand my rights clearly. When I signed off on each of the company accounts, I knew what I was doing. There is no way that I want Beadle to represent me."

If it weren't for her facial muscles, Abi's jaw would have broken loose and hit the desk.

❖

The interview suite was booked urgently. The cozy chat with Tracy had moved into more serious territory and this needed to be officially recorded.

Abi and Bob conducted the meeting, they both had started to gain an understanding of the operation and felt best qualified to dig deeper. Despite Tracy's insistence on not wanting a lawyer present, Abi convinced her to have one in the room. A quick phonecall and Cora Middleton, the appointed solicitor, sat with Tracy for 30 minutes prior to the interview. Tracy seemed clear and determined; her shoulders had noticeably lifted.

Tracy was read her rights. It was made clear that, at this stage, she was not a suspect or charged with anything, but everything that was discussed in this session could be used as evidence against her. It was also explained, as the meeting was recorded, that the solicitor sitting with her was there to represent her best interests and ensure that the interview was conducted correctly.

"So, are you happy to proceed, Tracy?"

She looked over at the solicitor, who nodded in approval and the interview began.

Outside the interview room, separated by a one way mirror, sat Tom and Chris. Chris was taking copious notes, Tom simply listened - everything was recorded and he had developed, over 30 years of policing, the ability to retain the key information.

The interview covered the myriad of companies set up by Williams. Tracy was sure that there must be others, the money left her sight at a couple of places, but she didn't do the accounting for them

Although the files would soon be subject to forensic evaluation (the court order came through just before the meeting started) she was keen to demonstrate a couple of the rabbit warrens she had created.

After two hours, the interview concluded for the day. Tracy was thanked for her honesty. Her solicitor had told her on many occasions that she was incriminating herself, but she was adamant that she would continue. A follow up meeting would be called shortly. It was strongly recommended that Tracy speak to no one, her solicitor nodded in response, and Tracy accepted.

"You have my word," short and to the point.

"Well, this opens a whole can of worms. Tracy has a story to tell, but where does this help us with the investigation into Sally's death?"

The other three looked at Tom, they all knew how each part of the puzzle looked. The suspicion was that Sally uncovered accounting issues that may have led to her death, but no one could prove this. Each bit of evidence was incriminating, but until they linked them, there would be no way to help solve her murder.

"Ok, can I try and say what we do know?" Chris looked around the team for approval, which they acknowledged. "I don't think Gordon killed his wife and all the time we keep him inside with no evidence, I think we're leaving ourselves exposed. I say we let him go. For now."

No one disagreed. Tom spoke.

"I agree, I suggest we go over there in a couple of hours and release him under police bail."

Two hours later, Tom noticed the time when he made his statement, he called over to Chris.

"Come on son, it's time to release him. Do you want to call Beadle and get him over to Lewes prison? I'll call the governor and let him know that he will have a spare cell tonight."

Chris dialled from his mobile, it was answered after one ring.

"Detective Thomas, so lovely to hear from you. How may I help?"

"Mr. Beadle, I was wondering if you could meet us at Lewes Prison. We intend to release Mr. Gordon under police bail, we need you there to complete the necessary paperwork. How soon can you get over?"

"Well, I'm actually on the course in Lewes. I'm four putts down and have three holes to go. Maybe now is a good time to call it a day, I think that allows me to call it a draw."

"If you only have three holes to go, I suggest that you complete the round. See you there in," Chris glanced at the clock, 'let's say 55 minutes at 17.30."

"I will be delighted, see you then."

Chris ended the call, his teeth gritted. He had been played all the way through this investigation, and Beadle held the strings. He wandered over to Tom.

"All set for 17.30 boss."

"How was he?"

"In what way? He was very celebratory in his tone, if that's what you mean?"

"So he wasn't agitated?"

"No." Strange question, Chris thought, and then the penny dropped, "Of course, you left it two hours to see if Tracy Pointer had called Beadle. Nope, she hasn't called at all."

"That's what I thought, just wanted to be sure. Pointer will make a solid witness, Beadle doesn't know how much shit is going to come his way, I'm not sure what his involvement is with Williams, but I think he will be busy for quite a few months. It's a shame that we won't be able to investigate him, but the fraud squad will have their day. Think of it as a victory, son. Anyhow, let's head over to Lewes now, get there before Beadle."

Parking comes at a premium at Lewes Prison, especially around 17.30. At this time of day most of the prison officers are present, and, as few can afford to live local to Lewes, most drive in. The car park was full. Thankfully, the police have their own spot right by the main gate. Beadle would have to park on a side street and walk up.

They were expected and led straight through to Gordon, who was waiting in an interview room. They walked in, said hello, and then sat there in an uncomfortable silence.

Beadle arrived at the gate by 17.15; he must have walked away from the game of golf and taken the draw. By some unwritten rule between the police and prison staff, solicitors were always kept waiting. Beadle's frustration was clear by the time he was led into the room at 17.40. Small victories.

"Welcome, Mr. Beadle. Would you like some time with your client before we begin? Tell you what, I'll grab us some coffee, we'll be back in five minutes," Chris offered the coffee through gritted teeth.

"Coffee would be wonderful, thanks. I'm straight off the course and a little thirsty. Black, no sugar." Beadle looked to James Gordon, who nodded, "and the same for James please."

Five minutes later, they came back into the room. It was apparent from the demeanour of both parties that the good news had already been shared. Gordon was clearly grinning.

"Right, straight to the point. We are going to let you go for now. You will be released on police bail. We have prepared a document here that explains what this means. I am sure that Mr. Beadle can explain the details," Tom looked at Beadle who was sipping his coffee, he nodded his confirmation.

"To be absolutely clear, you've not been totally released. There are certain obligations on your part. You will need to report to a police station every 24 hours. We request that you stay in the vicinity of Lewes and apply for permission to leave within a 10 mile radius of your home. You should not talk to the press. And, and I make this very clear, you are still under arrest on suspicion of the murder of your wife Sally Gordon. Do you have any questions?"

Beadle answered, "No, that will be fine Detective Inspector."

Tom passed the paperwork over to Beadle who perused the document and indicated to Gordon where to sign. Chris noted how Gordon signed with his left hand.

Beadle passed the document back to Tom and then stood up.

"Thank you Gentleman, could you escort me to the gate please. I'm sure that my client will be keen to get back to normality as soon as possible."

"Follow me," Tom stood up and walked to the door.

"I'll catch you up in five minutes boss, need to collect my thoughts. It's been a long day. It's been a long week," Chris looked over at Tom as he spoke.

Tom could sense the despondency, all detectives have to experience the ones that got away, sad that his first real case had ended this way,

"No problem son. I'll be waiting by the gate," Tom left with the other two, did he detect a smile of victory on the lips of Beadle?

The car ride back to the station was in silence.

"You've had a long day son, there will be others. Don't let it get to you. Drop off your stuff and get yourself home. Are you on duty this weekend?" Tom broke the silence as he looked over at Chris.

"Yes"

"More reason to get yourself home."

They returned to the station and Chris went straight to his desk. Abi had already left, it must have been a long day for her to leave so soon. He logged onto his computer and picked up the phone. He could see Tom's disapproval.

"Five minutes, that's all. I Just need to tie up a few loose ends."

Tom nodded. He checked Chris's desk ten minutes later and he was gone.

Chapter Eleven

Text to Carl

"Sorry for the delay in getting back to you. Today has been a crazy day, a police officer's life, I suppose. So lovely to see you last night. Sorry the night before last, told you it was a crazy day :-). Can I cook you dinner on Wednesday. My 14 day shift finishes so I definitely don't have work in the morning ;-) Chris x

Text toAbi

"Abi, are you planning to interview Tracy tomorrow? I would like to ask her a few questions before we are forced to hand this to the fraud squad"

Text from Abi

"What the fuck Chris. It's 4AM! Why are you awake? And what's this about the fraud squad? It's our case, I'll be fucked if I'm going to hand this over"

Text from Carl

"It's a date. X"

Text to Abi

"It's 4AM and you're still awake? Maybe I should ask? Oh, I have guessed. Say hello to Roger from me. Boss told me the case will be going to Fraud, we only have this weekend. Can you set something up for tomorrow afternoon and let me sit in?"

Text from Abi

"Roger says hello and we're both happy you have a date for Wednesday. You do know when you say you're not working the following morning that's an implicit invitation to breakfast? :-) I'll set something up for the afternoon"

Text to Abi

"Implicit? Explicit? Who cares ;-) Make it around 3 p.m., no earlier. I'll explain later. Sleep well. Or don't, your choice ;-)"

Considering the previous day both had and the lack of sleep both evidently experienced, Abi and Chris were at their desks looking sprightly.

"What's with the fraud squad?" Abi's first question. Chris was expecting this.

"It's not our area of expertise. We have only been ploughing through invoices and details because it was part of a murder investigation. This is going to require a lot more forensic accounting, way beyond our skill set. I think we both realise this is money laundering on a huge scale. Do you recall the training on laundering and how there are various tentacles that span multiple companies, all designed to hide the source and destination of the money? I think we have uncovered one tentacle, that's all Do you want to spend all the time plugging through spreadsheets and invoices?"

Chris looked at Abi as he spoke, she was sharing the despondency he felt the day before. She didn't reply.

"No, I didn't think so. Let's get Tracy in again today and see if we can get some understanding of who Williams is. He is starting to sound a bit like Charlie in Charlie's Angels"

"The film? What do you mean?"

Chris started to realise just how absorbed he had been with the DVD collection, Abi would need to watch the full TV series to realise how Charlie never makes an appearance. She'd obviously missed the connection.

"It doesn't matter. Let's setup the interview and take it from there. Can we aim for around 3 p.m?"

"Yes, you said so last night. I'll sort something out. Should we tell the boss?"

"Oh, he'll be in shortly. I know it's his day off, but he'll be in."

The day was one of documentation. Documenting the interview with Tracy, the session with Gordon and Beadle. Documenting the meal times. If it wasn't on paper (or on a computer) it didn't exist, and it never happened. It's pointless referring to a phone call as evidence in two weeks time if, as far as the paper trail goes, it didn't happen.

"Sandwich?" Abi spoke and Chris lifted his head from the computer.

"Sure, a cheese and onion sandwich, please."

"I'm not your servant, I was asking you if you would like to come with me to get a sandwich?"

Chris looked at his phone, something he had been doing all morning, willing it to ring.

"Sorry, no. I'll skip," he said as he buried his head into the computer and glanced again at the phone.

Ten minutes later Abi returned, she threw the sandwich at him.

"You owe me."

No response

"Thank you would be appropriate."

Still no response.

❖

As expected, Tom arrived just before the interview with Tracy.

"What's happening, guys. I sensed something was up. This copper's nose had better go after I retire otherwise it will be a miserable affair."

"I hear you'll be transferring the Tracy Pointer stuff to Fraud on Monday?" She looked in Tom's eyes hoping the pitiful look might make him change his mind.

"Sorry, Abi. Yes Fraud will be in Monday and take away all the files. It's too big for us; I have a suspicion the tentacles go far and wide."

"Chris has told me all about the tentacles, we've all been on the same course."

"Yes, we have, and that's about it. These guys know more about accounting fraud than we will ever know about homicide, we'll have to let it go," Tom was quite firm. Quite an admission from a

Detective Inspector with over 30 year's service.

"Yes, I figured. Anyhow, I wanted to plug Tracy to see if we could get any more information on Williams. We've only got the two days."

"Copper's nose again. I thought that was happening. We'll make a detective out of you yet."

He looked over at Chris, his eyes were focused on the telephone. He looked anxious. Abi's phone rang, Tracy was in reception with her solicitor.

"That's Tracy, I'll go get her now," Abi called over to Chris. No response. She went to reception.

Chris's phone rang, he picked it up immediately.

"Yes? Uh um. Yes. YES! I fucking owe you mate."

He slammed the phone and punched the air. Abi was leading Tracy into the interview room and chose to ignore Chris. Tom was a bit more concerned, he walked over.

Ten minutes later, Chris and Tom joined them in the interview suite. The interview hadn't started. As agreed with Tom, Chris walked in and Tom watched through the windows.

Abi re-read her rights and signalled the interview had started.

Abi led the interview, she was asking questions about how the companies were setup (on the internet), her contact with Williams (exclusively email), and the postal addresses of the companies (all

PO boxes or equivalent).

Tracy was the perfect interviewee. She answered all questions clearly and concisely and offered information that wasn't asked of her. For example; she registered four companies that didn't appear to be part of Williams' sphere but recognised connections in the postal addresses. She had catalogued all the companies in a single page under headings; Williams declared, Williams not declared, and Williams suspected. Her evidence would be gold dust to the fraud police as they expanded their investigations.

The only time that she became anxious was when they mentioned Beadle. He came across as Williams' enforcer. Once she suspected a company was linked to a Williams company and emailed him to request more information, Beadle was around within the hour, ignorant of normal business etiquette and demanding details of how she had assumed such a thing. Each time he was aggressive and demanding, so she chose to keep these visits to an absolute minimum. Beadle would have been the obvious choice for her defence; he was effectively on the same payroll, but she detested the man with a vengeance,

"Tracy, I'm going to ask something of you now. I don't want you to be worried. You're safe here, and you have the full protection of the law."

Abi gave Chris a sideways glance. He had been silent up until this point, and his question suggested that the interview was changing direction in a way that she didn't understand. He moved his hand and squeezed Abi's arm in reassurance.

"Tracy, I know you don't want to speak about Beadle and you certainly don't want him near you. Please be assured, we understand and have your safety as our main concern. You won't come to any harm."

His voice was low and comforting, a side that Abi had not experienced in the meetings, she knew him personally and knew he was capable of empathy, but at work he was an auto-mon, just focused on the job at hand.

Tracy nodded. She felt instant empathy and was ready to respond. And then Chris hit her with the request.

"Tracy," he also looked at the solicitor for reassurance, "I want you to call Beadle and let him know you're being interviewed about Williams' companies."

Her face went white and her head started to shake aggressively.

"No, no. I can't. Look, I'm too deep in this, I want out. I know that I have done wrong, but I don't want to see Beadle ever again. He's a part of this. A big part. He has contacts, and he told me. I can't trust you and your support."

Tom was watching from outside of the room, he was expecting Chris's request and Tracy's response. He was impressed by the way Chris was handling this. If he had any doubts, he would have walked in on the interview and used his experience to achieve the same. But, no, Chris was doing alright.

"If I could have a few words with my client, please," the solicitor, mostly silent up until this point, recognised the distress and called a halt.

"Of course," Abi stared at the clock, "interview terminated at 15.45." The same time that she pressed the stop button, the sound from the room piped to Tom outside ceased. They had to respect the solicitor/client confidentiality. Chris and Abi walked out to see Tom.

"Good work Chris, I think she'll go for it."

"Anyone want to tell me what was happening here?" Had it been just Chris playing this game, Abi would have used stronger language, but she realised she was part of a greater plan and felt strangely happy.

Chris explained.

The solicitor signalled; she knew the mirror was one way and implicitly accepted that she was not being listened to, even solicitors have to accept the word of the police sometimes. Chris and Abi re-entered the room.

"My client will agree to your request, but she has a demand that she doesn't have to see Beadle without her prior approval. She also wants assurances of her safety."

As she spoke the word 'safety' Tom walked in.

"Detective Inspector Christoper. You have my word." Tom looked Tracy in the eye as he spoke the words with such authority that neither Tracy nor Cora, her solicitor, even questioned them nor requested written confirmation. He was obviously an old school detective who had trust written through his core.

Cora looked at Tracy and then spoke again.

"OK, what do you want Tracy to do?" The change from 'my client' to 'Tracy' was deliberate. This was no longer about her client, Tracy was helping the police outside of her own domain.

"Would you mind putting your phone on speaker, Tracy? I just want you to repeat the following words." He passed her a piece of paper, there were only a couple of sentences,

"What if he asks questions?"

"He won't," Chris said quite firmly.

She found his number in the phone book and dialled, selecting the speaker as it connected and hearing the first ring.

"Beadle. What's up?"

"I'm at the station. The police are asking me about Sound Transport Services."

"Don't say another word. I'm on my way. East Street station?"

"Yes."

He disconnected. They looked at the clock, 15.57.

"Tracy, we have facilities to keep you safe. We can take you over there straight away or if you need to collect something we can go via your home. You'll be safe. You have my word." Again Tom's reassuring manner exuded trust.

"We have a specialist officer, she will be through in a few minutes. She will explain everything to you," no sooner had Tom spoke than a plain clothes officer entered the room and took Tracy's arm.

"Tracy, my name is Barbara. Shall we chat?" She led Tracy out of the office. Both Chris and Abi would comment afterwards how relaxed Tracy seemed, as if the world's problems had been lifted from her shoulders.

"What next?" Abi started to talk but Chris beat her to it.

"What next? We wait. I don't think we will have to wait long."

❖

It took Beadle exactly 13 minutes to get to his car, drive over and park up. They suspected he had parked on the double yellows outside the station.

Chris went to the reception and collected Beadle, the amicable charm he had experienced in his last meting was gone totally. Every sinew of his body yelled livid. Chris decided against small talk and walked to the interview room.

Beadle's breath smelled of alcohol. Maybe they should alert traffic as well? No, it was the least of his problems.

As they entered, Beadle spoke.

"Can you leave me alone with …. Where is my client?"

"Please sit down, Mr. Beadle," As Tom was the senior officer, it was agreed that he would lead the meeting. Chris and Abi knew their roles and kept quiet.

"Where is my client? I demand to speak to my client."

"Mr. Beadle, we need to talk to you first of all. Your client has implicated you, and we want to discuss these allegations."

"I demand I talk to my client. These allegations will be struck off. Did she have a solicitor present, if not the sessions are null and void. I demand …" Beadle voice was raised, he was clearly confused with the way that events were moving.

"Please sit. In answer to your question, yes, she had a solicitor present throughout. The whole process is well above board. But we are not here to talk about your client. We are here to talk about you"

All three of them had met Beadle on multiple occasions and seen how he dominated the meetings throughout. He was in control. Just then, maybe it was temporary, but just then his confidence dropped and he sank into his chair.

"My first question is do you want to have a solicitor present? If don't have a solicitor, we can appoint one for you."

"No I don't need a fucking solicitor. What the fuck is this about?"

Abi inserted two cassettes and pressed record.

"You do not have to say anything. But, it may harm your defence if you do not mention when questioned something which you later rely on in court. Anything you do say may be given in evidence. Are you happy for the interview to begin?" The words spoken by Tom were as common to Beadle as the Lord's Prayer, but he had never heard them directed at him.

"Can someone explain to me what is going on here?"

"I will repeat the question, do you want to have a solicitor present during this interview?"

"No, I fucking don't, will someone explain?"

Tom stared at Abi who started to talk.

"Mr. Beadle, we have recently interviewed Tracy Pointer. Can you confirm that you know who this person is?"

"Tracy Pointer is my client. I should be talking to her now. Her submission is inadmissible because I, as her solicitor, was not present. I demand to be able to talk to my client. NOW!"

"Miss Pointer has provided details of Sound Transport Services, Wick Consultancy, …"

Abi listed the companies one by one. A deliberate pause between each name, just long enough for each nail to be driven into Beadle's body. He reacted with a wince as each name was read out.

"Yes, I am aware of these companies. I am the appointed solicitor for each of these, my client, Kevin Williams, runs these companies, and I am his personal solicitor.

No one expected Williams' name to come up so quickly. But there it was. Time to press on.

"Many of these organisations are linked to the others, payments from one go to another and back again."

"And, is this illegal? If there is a valid reason for one company to invoice another, what is the issue? You have nothing. I am personally responsible as Mr. Williams' solicitor for the legal requirements of these companies and I demand to be able to speak to my client who is the accountant for these companies."

"Mr. Beadle, for the purpose of this interview, can you please explain how we have met previously?" Abi continued her tack.

"This is absurd. You know how we met. We have been meeting for the past week. I have been defending my client, James Gordon, over your absurd claims about him murdering his wife. You know all of this. James was released only yesterday. An innocent man, this is a conspiracy."

He stood up to leave. Tom signalled him to sit down.

"You are well aware that Mr. Gordon was not released. He is still under suspicion and subject to police bail. I shouldn't have to explain this to you," It was a cheap shot, but boy, Tom enjoyed using it. He continued.

"On Thursday I spoke to the CPS representative. I have been in this job for over 30 years and I hope to retire very soon. I have seen all the criminal solicitors in Sussex in my time. Every one. I have watched them progress from being snooty nosed kids fresh out of university to bloody good solicitors; some of whom are a match for me, I have to admit. But I had never met you before. Neither had the CPS lawyer. Don't you think that is strange?"

"Are you doubting my credentials, Detective Inspector? I qualified as a solicitor around the same time that you entered police college as a cadet. I have been practising law for longer than you have held your warrant card."

"Sir, I do not dispute your credentials. I have checked, and I can confirm your dates."

"Do you watch 80s films, Mr. Beadle?" Chris spoke for the first time.

"What? What the fuck are you on about?"

"Simple question, do you watch 80's films?"

"What has this got to do with anything? Yes, I watch 80's films. What has this got to do with anything?"

"I love them. I've seen all of the classics, Dirty Dancing, An Officer and a Gentleman, Fatal Attraction. Love them all. I was born twenty years too late. Have you seen Jagged Edge?" The question asked by Chris was rhetorical, he didn't wait long enough for an answer.

"You see, Jeff Bridges' character is a rich millionaire, today, I suppose he would be a billionaire. He could afford the best lawyers on the planet, yet he chose to use the company lawyer who specialised in corporate law. She had never been in a criminal court before, let alone defended a murderer. Why did he do this?"

Another rhetorical question.

"It made me think, if I was charged with murder, why would I call a company solicitor to defend me?"

Not a rhetorical question, but no response to the question. So Chris continued.

"You know we checked Gordon's phone to see whom he had called, there were no phone calls after 9.40. There was a text sent to an unlisted number and another received from the same number. We can't find the text on the phone, it must have been deleted, but we do know that a text was sent. We can't see any phone calls on Saturday at all. We can see James texted his wife just after midnight, the message reads 'Pissed, pick me up, at HH now.' We can also confirm that he received a short call at 1.06 a.m., but no other calls that day. Until, of course, he called the police at just gone midnight."

"I'm still none the wiser what you are getting at. So I'm a corporate lawyer. I happen to know James through golf. He called me in desperation, maybe it was from the house phone? I assume you have checked?"

"We have checked all of the phones, Mr. Beadle. No calls made. Yet somehow he communicated to you that he needed your help and, wonder of wonders, you turned up within minutes of his arrival at the interview block. How can you explain this?"

"I don't know, maybe he has a phone that you don't know about? A business phone maybe? You're the investigation team. Why are you asking me? Look, we are talking about my client, what has this got to do with me?"

"In the film the character is found to be innocent, and his lawyer, played by Glenn Close, falls in love with him. A happy ending."

Beadle was noncommittal. Chris continued.

"And then, as she was putting away the laundry, she found the typewriter in the back of the airing cupboard, She hit the keys and knew he was guilty."

"Are you suggesting that my client's story can be made into a Hollywood film? This is absurd. Where is this going?"

"You see, at that point Jeff Bridge's character was found innocent. He would have gotten away with it but failed to tidy up after himself. If he had disposed of the typewriter, it would have been a happy ending"

"And quite frankly, a pointless film," Abi chipped in.

"Exactly a pointless film. So the past week we have been investigating Gordon as the suspect, and at every turn the evidence blew up in our face," did he detect a small smile from Beadle? Maybe, ok time to wipe off that smile.

"We were left with nothing, bar an uncorroborated confession.

278

Nothing. But the killer did leave a couple of trails. We have their fingerprints on the underside of the filing cabinet, a finger print on a plastic sheaf found in the garden, we think this came from the hockey stick that was implicated in the murder."

"We have already proven that this was not the murder weapon. It is wooden and unbruised. Carry on with your pointless discussion," Beadle said trying to take control of the discussion.

"Accepted, this wasn't the murder weapon. But we did find the murder weapon, tucked away on a country lane leading from the Offham Road to the Downs. A sand wedge, the club missing from Gordon's golf set. An exact match to the wound it inflicted. And a partial print that matches the other two."

All gamblers have a tell. They can be ice cold calm throughout a poker match, no one can read them, but they all have a tell, something in their demeanour that gives away the game. In the case of Beadle, his tell was not so subtle, he collapsed into his seat. All of his energy was expended. But Chris still had to deliver the killer punch. And he did it with relish.

"I hope you enjoyed your cup of coffee yesterday. After you left, I picked up the cup, actually all of the cups, and had them sent to forensics for analysis. I got the results at 14.45 today. Three of them matched; Detective Inspector Christoper, James Gordon and myself. The fourth matched the latent prints that we found on the murder weapon, the plastic sheaf and the underside of the drawer handle."

Beadle sunk lower in his seat.

"Mr Beadle, also known as Kevin Williams, you are charged with the murder of Sally Gordon. You do not have to say anything ……"

The words blurred.

.

Chapter Twelve

There are only three countries without a written constitution, Israel, New Zealand, and the UK. Countries with constitutions have to enact all laws in line with the text. Most get around this limitation by amending the constitution or simply tearing it up and starting again.

Despite the UK being one of these countries, there is one small section of the population that is protected by a form of constitution, the imprisoned population. Although somewhat limited in comparison to "common law rights" enjoyed by other subjects, it does spell out rights on visitors, meals, exercise and other areas that the rest of the population can only assume are their rights.

Kevin Williams was provided with a small book describing these rights as he collected his prison-issue uniform. He had previously undressed under the gaze of the Prison Officer who catalogued each item and placed it in a box that would be available for him to collect on his release. A doctor had performed a cavity search before he was allowed to dress in the uniform.

As someone more attuned to quality fashion and fabrics, he found the materials stiff and itchy, and the cut very plain.

"You'll have time to get used to it," the Prison Officer assured him. One of many humorous barbs he would have to experience.

Time, a word he had never contemplated before, at least not in this way. He recalled his frustration waiting for delayed planes or arriving late and apologetic to meetings. He suspected that the word was just about to take on a new meaning.

The plan he had agreed with, or rather forced upon, Gordon was to provide a cut-and-dry murder and then watch the evidence fall away piece by piece. His contact in the Argus welcomed the details of the failed evidence, just as the police were trying to understand it themselves.

Once released, he was going to put Gordon on a ferry to France before they found anything incriminating, a fake passport was ready, and he was due to catch the ferry within days. The police attention would have been on Gordon, a fugitive who had fled justice, and attention on Williams himself would simply float away.

Those junior detectives can go and fuck themselves, Thomson and Thomas. When he first met them, they were putty in his hands. He had totally misread them. Williams had to sit with his solicitor while they listed item after item of evidence that implicated him, not Gordon. Him!

Despite all of his precautions in avoiding social media and using his alter ego, Beadle, whenever he needed to come out of the dark, they managed to join the dots and implicate someone who had tried his best not to exist.

He had heard a lot about prison and the regime run by the prisoners and the arbitrary hierarchy established that was based on the crime. Paedophiles and child killers sat firmly at the bottom, bank robbers and cop killers at the top. The lower you were in the ranks, the more miserable your life would become. Try as he could, he didn't think that a cold blooded killer of a defenceless woman would endear him to other criminals. On the prison hierarchy, he was somewhere in the sewers.

All prisoners cry on their first night inside. All. Don't let anyone tell you any different; regardless of the person and the bravado they put on, as soon as that heavy metal door slams for the first time and the lights go out, the enormity of the situation hits them. Williams was no exception.

Like every fresh prisoner, he sought a friend, someone to make life a bit more bearable.

The first morning, the friend arrived.

"Mr. Williams," it was a statement, not a question. Williams had been sitting alone trying to avoid eye contact and figure out who was who.

"Hello. And who are you?"

"I'm your best friend, Mr. Williams. We have a mutual acquaintance who has asked me to keep an eye out for you. A lot of bad things can happen in prison, people fall down stairs, they put too much sugar in their hot drink and accidentally spill it on themselves, they get their fingers trapped in the door hinges, they slip on the soap in the shower and knock out all of their teeth. I could go on, but this place is a health and safety nightmare. We wouldn't want you to get hurt, would we?"

Williams nodded, his mouth was too dry to answer. He suspected the list of health and safety violations was a lot longer than those provided by his new friend.

"You see, our acquaintance wants me to look out for you. You see, he's concerned that your mutual business dealings might come up in questioning. He wants you to know that if the police suggest a reduced sentence for information, they are bluffing. You see, you're in here for murder, the best they can do is trim a couple of months off a very long sentence. So he just wants me to let you know that you have someone keeping an eye out for you while you are inside.

I have a very special eye, I'm a caring sort of person. Have a good day, Mr. Williams and, if you want anything, let me know and I will do what I can. I think we're going to be great friends."

Printed in Great Britain
by Amazon

27403037R00159